圖解廣東話 2

tou4 gaai2 gwong2 dung1 waa2

阿塗 編繪
七刻 編譯

compiled & illustrated by **Ah To**
edited & translated by **Chukhak**

Cantonese2.jpg

目錄
Contents

圖解説明
Guide to the Book

❶ 粵拼
（香港語言學學會粵語拼音方案）
Jyutping
(LSHK Cantonese Romanisation Scheme)

❷ 廣東話俗語
Cantonese colloquial expression

❸ 直譯原文
Literal translation

❹ 插圖
Illustration

❺ 中文解釋
Chinese explanation

❻ 意譯原文
Sense-for-sense translation

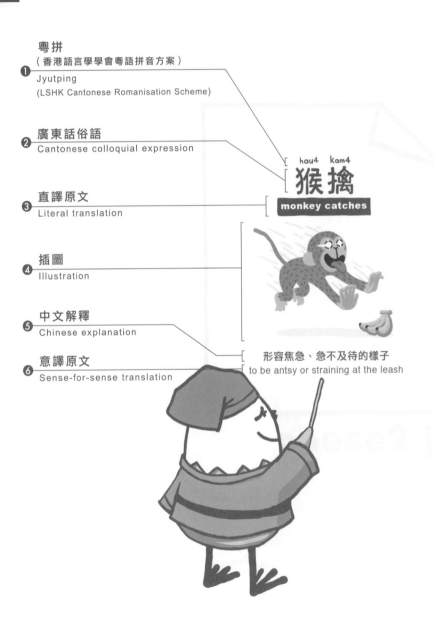

hau4 kam4

猴擒

monkey catches

形容焦急、急不及待的樣子
to be antsy or straining at the leash

zuk1　zik1　aap3　　mou5　Sam1　gon1

竹織鴨 > 冇心肝

bamboo-woven duck > no heart and liver

歇後語
a two-part
allegorical saying

沒心肝的人：形容人沒有感情；
或對別人的要事不上心、無心裝載
a heartless person ; an absent-minded person
who is negligent or indifferent to others' important matters

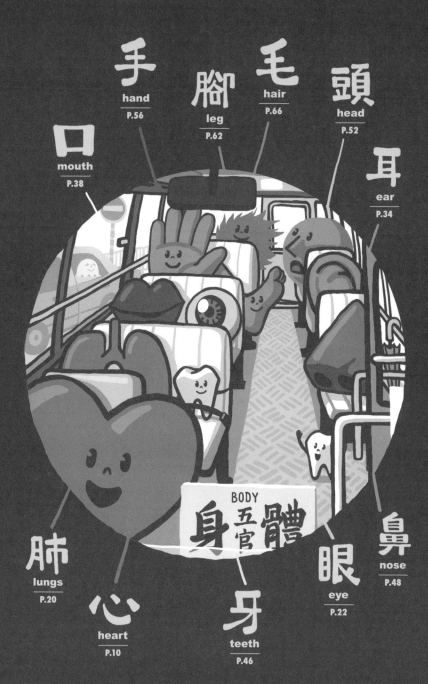

手
hand
P.56

腳
leg
P.62

毛
hair
P.66

頭
head
P.52

口
mouth
P.38

耳
ear
P.34

BODY
身五官體

肺
lungs
P.20

心
heart
P.10

牙
teeth
P.46

眼
eye
P.22

鼻
nose
P.48

heart.jpg

gik1 Sam1
激 心
irritated heart

因對某人失望而感到氣憤和悲傷
to be enraged and saddened
when being disappointed by someone

0443

faa1 Sam1
花 心
flowery heart

對愛情不專一
to be fickle and untrustworthy as a lover ;
to play the field

0444

mo6 Sam1
磨 心
grindstone's heart (pivot)

磨的中軸：比喻替意見不同的人
做調停而左右為難，感覺受氣
a person who is caught between a rock and
a hard place when being a negotiator
between two opposing persons or parties

0445

bo1 lei1 Sam1
玻 璃 心
glassy heart

形容人內心過度脆弱敏感、
容易受打擊
snowflake
– an overly sensitive
or easily offended person

0446

心 涼
Sam1 loeng4

heart cool

當知道仇人或競爭者不幸時，
幸災樂禍而心感痛快
to rejoice and gloat over one's enemy's
or rival's misfortune

0447

心 寒
Sam1 hon4

heart chilled

心裏覺得可怕
to feel a blood-chilling horror ;
to be sent a chill in one's heart

0448

心 悒
Sam1 ngap1

heart depressed

鬧心：內心不安、鬱結
to be upset and worried

0449

心 散
Sam1 saan2

heart scattered

做事不專心，心神渙散
to be easily distracted,
unable to concentrate

0450

Sam1 jyun5

心 軟
heart softened

經不起別人的懇求而動搖，
產生同情或憐憫
to give in to somebody's plea ;
to have a soft spot for someone

0451

Sam1 taam5

心 淡
heart diluted

對某人或某事心灰意冷或氣餒
to be dismayed at someone or something
and show indifference

0452

Sam1 ziu3

心 照
heart shines

彼此心裏明白而不必明説
to have a tacit understanding
between two persons

0453

Sam1 gei1

心 機
heart machine

做事的耐心、心神
one's patience and efforts
paid in doing something

0454

Sam1 gwaa3 gwaa3
心掛掛
heart (keeps on) hanging hanging

心裏經常惦念、老想着
to be concerned about someone
or something and think about that all the time

0455

Sam1 si1 si1
心思思
heart (keeps on) thinking thinking

老是惦記着、想去做某事情
to be obsessed with something ;
to feel tempted to do something

0456

Sam1 do1 do1
心多多
hearts many many

做事的興致或興趣容易轉移；
既貪心又三心兩意
to be full of whims, wanting to do
many things at the same time ;
to be greedy and yet indecisive

0457

Sam1 juk1 juk1
心郁郁
heart (keeps on) moving moving

心癢癢：
動了心想做某事，但還未行動
to be itching to do something

0458

14

Sam1 tau4 gou1

心頭高

heart head high

不安於現狀，志向（太）高
to be ambitious
and set one's goal (too) high

0459

Sam1 hyut3 siu2

心血少

heart blood deficient

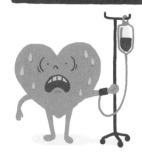

本來就心虛膽怯的人，
不能再受更多的驚嚇
someone who is easily flustered
and nervous cannot be further frightened

0460

---

hou2 Sam1 dei2

好心地

good heart base

心很善良
to be kind-hearted

0461

---

ding2 Sam1 caam3

頂心杉

**press against heart
the chinese fir**

眼中釘：事事與自己對着幹的人，
尤指頂撞、不聽話的子女
a thorn in one's flesh – an argumentative
person who crosses someone in almost
everything, esp. referring to a recalcitrant child

0462

15

Sam1 seoi2 cing1
心水清
heart water clear

頭腦清楚，不易被矇騙，
能注意到易被人忽略的事
to be observant to notice something
neglected by all others ; to be astute and
vigilant, hence not to be easily fooled

0463

Sam1 fo2 sing6
心火盛
heart fire burning fiercely

煩躁易怒
to be irritable

0464

dip6 maai4 Sam1 seoi2
疊埋心水
fold up heart water

放棄遊思妄想，收拾心情，
一心一意去做某事
to stop indulging in flights of fancy
and try to concentrate on doing one thing ;
to make up one's mind to do something

0465

Sam1 zung1 jau5 sou3
心中有數
**in (one's) heart (he)
has a count**

對情況和問題有基本了解，
對處理事情有一定的把握
to have a grasp of the situation
and know fairly well what to do

0466

Sam1 daai6 Sam1 sai3
心大心細
heart big heart small

猶豫不決
to be hesitant and double-minded

0467

dik1 hei2 Sam1 gon1
的(拘)起心肝
pick up heart liver

發奮、決心並努力去做某事
to be determined to do something
and make a serious effort to act on it

0468

hung1 Sam1 lou5 gun1
空心老倌
**empty heart (heartless)
cantonese opera artist**

表面看似有錢人，實是虛有其表、
裝富有的騙子；外強中乾、華而不實的人
a love scammer who pretends to be rich with a
luxurious lifestyle ; a fellow of vain pretension

0469

go3 Sam1 lei4 jat1 lei4
個心離一離
**the heart left (the body)
for a bit**

一下子嚇得要死
one's heart misses a beat ;
scare the pants off someone

0470

hou2 Sam1 zoek6 leoi4 pek3

好心着雷劈

**good heart
getting struck by thunder**

熱臉碰着冷屁股：熱心助人、
待人好，別人卻不買賬，反被怪責
one's kindness is not appreciated,
but is rejected or even resented instead

0471

loeng4 Sam1 dong3 gau2 fai3

良心當狗肺

**good heart is treated
as dog lung**

意近「好心着雷劈」：善心不被欣
賞，反遭拒絕、浪費甚或踐踏
one's good intention is not appreciated
but is treated as waste instead

0472

Sam1 beng6

心病

heart sickness

人與人之間心中不和
the covert conflict
or discontent among people

0473

zuk1 zik1 aap2　mou5 Sam1 gon1

竹織鴨 〉冇心肝

bamboo-woven duck > no heart and liver

沒心肝的人：形容人沒有感情；
或對別人的要事不上心、無心裝載
a heartless person ; an absent-minded person who is
negligent or indifferent to others' important matters

0474

m4　hai6　nei5　Sam1　jap6　min6　tiu4　cung4

唔係你心入面條蟲

not the worm in your heart

比喻自己根本不可能知道對方心中想法
"I am not your mind reader"
– to express how unreasonable it is to expect others
to discern your thoughts without you telling them

0475

---

jan4　jiu3　heoi1　Sam1　　fo2　jiu3　hung1　Sam1

人要虛心，火要空心

man needs a modest heart, fire needs an empty centre

做人要虛心學習才能獲得更多知識，
好比灶火要把柴架空，火才燒得旺盛
one needs to be humble to make progress,
like a fire on a hollow and roomy wood scaffolding would burn vigorously

0476

lungs.jpg

ziu3 fai3
照肺
X-ray the lungs

胸肺X光檢查：引申指員工被老闆
叫進辦公室訓話斥責，好比病人接
受醫生檢查，要忍着呼吸不能作聲
to take a chest radiograph ; to be scolded
or rebuked by one's boss or superior

0477

dou3 hau4 m4 dou3 fai3
到喉唔到肺
reached the throat but not the lungs

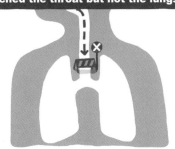

只去到喉嚨去不到肺部：意猶未盡，
只滿足了一半，感覺「吊癮」、吊胃口
to be just half satisfied ;
to have someone's enjoyment left in suspense

0478

jung6 go3 fai3 gong2 je5
用個肺講嘢
use the lungs to talk

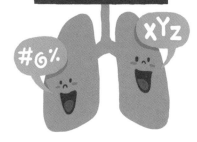

取「肺」的諧音「廢」，
即「說廢話」，胡說八道
to describe someone talking rubbish
or nonsense ; tautology, empty talk,
as「肺」(lung) and「廢」(useless)
are homophones in Cantonese

0479

jiu1 sam1 jiu1 fai3
夭心夭肺
bending heart bending lungs

被人頂撞、說中要害而心情不暢快；
對某些情景或說話特別有共鳴，戳中心扉
one gets hurt when others hit the nail on the head
by pointing out his flaws ; to describe the feeling of
a scene or artistic work resonating with someone
deep in the heart

0480

eye.jpg

ngaan5 faa1 faa1
眼花花
eyes flower flower

眼睛昏花，看東西模糊不清
to have a dull eyesight or blurred vision

0481

ngaan5 gwong1 gwong1
眼光光
eyes bright bright

失眠、睡不着
to have trouble falling asleep

0482

ngaan5 hung4 hung4
眼紅紅
eyes red red

哭得雙眼通紅
to be tearful ;
eyes turn red from crying

0483

ngaan5 baak6 baak6
眼白白
eyes white white (in vain)

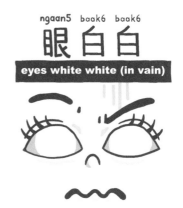

眼巴巴：只能無助地看着
不如意的事發生，卻未能阻止
to watch helplessly as something bad happens
but one cannot do anything about it

0484

23

ngaan5 zung1 deng1
眼中釘
nail in the eye

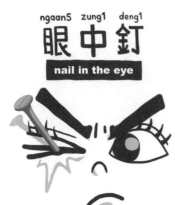

比喻心中最厭惡、痛恨的人，
如眼中釘一樣，只想除之而後快
to consider someone as an eyesore,
a thorn in one's flesh

0485

ngaan5 gok3 gou1
眼角高
eyes' corner high

眼睛長在腦門上：要求太高，不容易
看上眼，多形容人選伴侶時很挑剔
to be picky, choosy or having high
requirements, mostly used to refer to people
having a long list of criteria for an ideal spouse

0486

fo2 ze1 ngaan5
火遮眼
fire covers eyes

因過度生氣
而失去應有的理智
to be too angry to control oneself

0487

ngaan5 fo2 baau3
眼火爆
eyes fire bursts

一看見某些不當的行為或事情
便即火冒三丈
eyes blazing with anger
– to fly into a rage at seeing
something detestable

0488

gin3 cin2 hoi1 ngaan5
見錢開眼

see money open eyes

一看到錢財就睜大眼睛、
精神百倍：形容人貪財

to feel excited when being offered money ;
to be money-minded,
having an itchy palm

0489

jat1 ngaan5 gwaan1 cat1
一眼關七

**one eye looking at
seven (directions)**

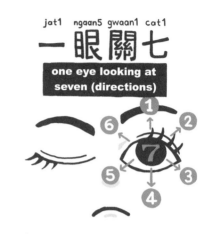

同時關顧前後左右上中下七個方位，指走
路時高度靈敏，同時兼顧多方面的狀況

to keep one's eyes peeled and be on the alert,
as the idiom literally means being attentive
to seven directions (front, back, left, right,
above, centre and below)

0490

jau5 ngaan5 gwong1
有眼光

possess eyes light

具有鑑賞識別的能力

to have an eye for something ;
to be discerning and have good taste

0491

mou5 ngaan5 tai2
冇眼睇

no eyes see

感嘆對某事情看不下去；
不想再理會某事

to be unable to bear (the sight of) something
anymore ; to refuse to be further involved ;
to give up on someone or something

0492

zek3 ngaan5 hoi1 zek3 ngaan5 bai3
隻眼開隻眼閉
one eye open one eye shut

遇事隱忍，得過且過，
採取視若無睹的迴避態度
to turn a blind eye to something ;
to choose not to interfere with or take
any action on something undesirable

0493

gin3 ngaa4 m4 gin3 ngaan5
見牙唔見眼
see the teeth, can't see the eyes

張口大笑
to grin, smile or beam from ear to ear

0494

sei3 ngaan5 zai2
四眼仔
four eyes boy

戴眼鏡的男子
a guy who wears glasses

0495

Sau2 baan2 ngaan5 gin3 gung1 fu1
手板眼見工夫
palm (touchable and) visible work

不需太多技巧、輕而易舉、
看看就能上手的工作
an easy task or job that does not take long
and does not require any special skills or talents

0496

haang4 lou6 m4 daai3 ngaan5
行路唔帶眼
walk on the road without bringing (one's) eyes

走路時不看路：
用於指責對方走路時碰撞到自己
to not pay attention to the surrounding when one
is on the go ; it is used for chiding someone for
accidentally bumping into you

0497

daai3 ngaan5 sik1 jan4
帶眼識人
bring eyes to meet people

小心交友，認清好人與壞人
to warn someone to be mindful
and discreet when making new friends

0498

saat3 jan4 m4 zaam2 ngaan5
殺人唔眨眼
kill people without blinking an eye

形容人極其心狠手辣
a cold-blooded murderer ;
to be bloodthirsty and ruthless

0499

nei5 ngaan5 mong6 ngo5 ngaan5
你眼望我眼
your eyes looking at my eyes

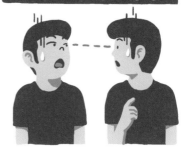

人們因驚訝或無奈而面面相覷，
不知如何是好
to look at each other in blank dismay,
not knowing what to do next

0500

ngau4 gam2 ngaan5
牛咁眼
cowlike eyes

睜大眼睛，聚精會神地注視着
to stare at someone or something,
eyes wide open without blinking

0501

baak6 gaap3 ngaan5
白鴿眼
white dove eyes

眼光勢利、瞧不起人
to describe someone as snobbish
and contemptuous of others

0502

dau3 gai 1 ngaan5
鬥雞眼
gamecock eyes

對眼：眼珠朝中間靠攏，
像兩隻雞搏鬥一樣
cross-eyed
(eyes misaligned inward)

0503

hung4 maau1 ngaan5
熊貓眼
panda eyes

睡眠不足所造成的黑眼圈
raccoon eyes
– dark circles, mainly caused
by sleep deprivation

0504

sik1 tai2 jan4 mei4 tau4 ngaan5 ngaak6
識睇人眉頭眼額

knowing how to read people's eyebrows, eyes and forehead

懂得掌握別人的脾性與心情，避免開罪別人

to be sensitive and keenly aware of others' temperament and emotions,
so as not to displease them

0505

---

maak3 daai6 ngaan5 gong2 daai6 waa6
擘大眼講大話

open wide the eyes to tell a lie

睜眼說瞎話：
指責某人赤裸裸的說謊，埋沒良心說自己也不相信的事

to lie through one's teeth ;
to blatantly lie in others' face

0506

tiu1 tung1 ngaan5 mei4
挑通眼眉
piercing through eyebrows

能看穿（挑通）別人的內心（眼眉）：
形容人精明，甚麼事都瞞不過他
a smart and sharp-witted person from whom
nothing can be hidden, as it literally means
someone can read others' mind by observing
their eye (and eyebrow) expressions

0507

tai3 jan4 ngaan5 mei4
剃人眼眉
shaving someone's eyebrows

故意使某人出醜、丟臉；
挫人傲氣
to humiliate someone, making him lose face ;
to take someone down a peg or two

0508

seoi2 zam3 ngaan5 mei4
水浸眼眉
**water soaking (flooding)
the eyebrows**

形容大禍臨頭了
（而某人還不醒悟）
to be in deadly haste or imminent danger
(but one still hasn't come to realize it)

0509

jat1 hok3 ngaan5 leoi6
一殼眼淚
a dipper of tears

形容事情令人感到辛酸或委屈，
現多指損失慘重的心情
to consider an experience to be
saddening and bitter ; to cry over one's loss

0510

眉精眼企
mei4 zing1 ngaan5 kei5

eyebrows refined and eyes upright

樣子精明又機靈
to look shrewd and smart

0511

眉飛色舞
mei4 fei1 sik1 mou5

eyebrows flying and colours (facial expression) dancing

形容人非常喜悅、得意洋洋的樣子，
興奮得滔滔不絕
to beam with joy ; to talk exultantly

0512

各花入各眼
gok3 faa1 jap6 gok3 ngaan5

different flowers enter (please) different eyes

蘿蔔青菜，各有所愛：
每個人的審美觀和喜好各有不同，實屬平常
different strokes for different folks ; to each his own ;
one man's meat is another man's poison

0513

天開眼
tin1 hoi1 ngaan5
heaven opens eyes

或「天有眼」：老天有眼，
報應分明，正義得到伸張
Heaven is a good judge – to get one's
comeuppance ; when the innocents are
vindicated or the wicked are punished

0514

跌眼鏡
dit3 ngaan5 geng2
dropping glasses

事情發展出乎意料，
或因估計錯誤而感到非常驚訝
to be taken aback or surprised by a wrong
prediction or an unexpected outcome

0515

眼闊肚窄
ngaan5 fut3 tou5 zaak3
eyes wide stomach narrow

形容人想吃或叫了很多東西，
實際上卻吃不下
to bite off more than one can chew ;
to overestimate one's appetite

0516

財不可露眼
coi4 bat1 ho2 lou6 ngaan5
money can't be exposed to eyes

錢財不好隨便在人前顯露，
以防引來劫匪
let not your valuables be easily seen
(to avoid being ripped off) ;
opportunity makes the thief

0517

tit3 goek3 maa5 ngaan5 san4 sin1 tou5

鐵腳馬眼神仙肚

iron legged, horse's eyes and immortal's stomach

體能好、能不睡不吃而辛勞工作的人，
多用以形容香港記者：多跑、熬夜、捱肚餓
an energetic person who can endure hard work by running around,
staying up all night and not eating for a very long time ;
to be considered as the three prerequisites for being a HK reporter

0518

---

daan1 ngaan5 lou2 tai2 lou5 po4   jat1 ngaan5 tai2 saai3

單眼佬睇老婆＞一眼睇晒

single-eyed man looks at his wife > one eye sees all

一覽無遺；一目了然；
空間太小或物件太少，一眼便已看盡
a panoramic view ; to describe something as too few,
too simple or too obvious that one can see or understand at a glance

0519

ear.jpg

ngaau5 ji5 zai2
咬耳仔
bite little ear

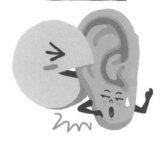

低聲耳語，説悄悄話
to whisper in someone's ear

0520

daai6 ji5 lung1
大耳窿
big ear hole

高利貸債權人：來源一説是昔日於街
市放數者會將銀錢塞進耳窿之中，
另一説是印巴裔放數者愛穿耳窿
戴大耳環，因而得名
a loan shark, a usurious moneylender

0521

mou5 ji5 sing3
冇耳性
having no ear's nature

形容人健忘
to be absent-minded or forgetful ;
to have a memory like a sieve

0522

seon6 fung1 ji5
順風耳
downwind ear

形容人聽力很好；
知道很多八卦傳聞的人
to have a good hearing ; a person
who is able to get wind of a lot of gossips

0523

35

ji5　zai2　jyun5
耳仔軟
little ear softened

為人心軟，容易聽信別人説話，
或是被人説服或影響
to be suggestible or credulous

0524

---

teng1　ceot1　ji5　jau4
聽出耳油
when hearing, the ear oil (earwax) comes out

形容音樂非常悦耳動聽
to express admiration for
a piece of beautiful music

0525

---

gaak3　coeng4　jau5　ji5
隔牆有耳
on the other side of the wall there is an ear

勸人説話小心以免洩露；
即使秘密商量，別人也可能知道
walls have ears – to beware of eavesdroppers ;
to suspect that a secret can never
be truly hidden

0526

---

dong3　ji5　bin1　fung1
當耳邊風
treating (it) as the wind (blowing) beside the ear

對別人的説話置之不理
to take no heed of one's words ;
to turn a deaf ear to
someone or something

0527

syu6 hei2 ji5 zai2
豎起耳仔
erect little ear

洗耳恭聽
to cock an ear at
someone or something

0528

waak6 zek3 ji5 soeng5 coeng4
畫隻耳上牆
draw an ear on the wall

罵小孩不聽話，像沒帶耳朵一般，
不把大人的話放在心上
to scold a child for not listening to grown-ups

0529

zo2 ji5 jap6 jau6 ji5 ceot1
左耳入右耳出
left ear in right ear out

出 EXIT　　入 ENTRANCE

形容人很快便忘了剛聽到的話
to go in one ear and out the other

0530

mouth.jpg

siu3 baau3 zeoi2
笑 爆 嘴
the laugh explodes the mouth

笑得要死；
某事或人差勁得令人發笑
to laugh one's head off ;
to consider someone or something to be lousy
enough to become the laughing stock

0531

jat1 leon2 zeoi2
一 輪 嘴
a round of mouths

一口氣急促講話，
別人都聽不清楚或沒有機會插嘴
to talk non-stop aggressively ; to speak too
fast that no one can hear what is said clearly
or there is no chance for anyone to interrupt

0532

ngaam1 zeoi2 jing4
啱 嘴 型
a good match of mouth types

二人談得很投機，志趣相投
to hit it off with someone ;
to have found like-minded
and congenial friends

0533

bok3 zeoi2 bok3 sit6
駁嘴駁舌
**retorting mouth
and retorting tongue**

形容人（尤其小孩）
每句話都要強辯頂嘴
an argumentative person (esp. referring to
one's child) who always talks back

0534

hoi1　hau2　gap6　zoek6　lei6

開口齡着脷

(as soon as) one opens his mouth he bites his tongue

形容人口沒遮攔，
一開口便説錯話或得罪人
to put one's foot in one's mouth ;
a person whose tongue runs riot
and says nothing right

0535

---

ngap1　dou3　zeoi2　seon4　bin1

嗑到嘴唇邊

speak (the words come up) to the lips' side

對一些事情有依稀印象，
但一時間無法完整地想起來
to have something on the tip of one's tongue

0536

---

tau1　sik6　m4　maat3　zeoi2

偷食唔抹嘴

sneaking food without wiping the mouth

偷做壞事卻沒有善後，最終被發現；
偷情後未有銷毀證據
to forget to cover up one's own plot which
is then discovered ; to forget destroying the
evidence after cheating on one's partner

0537

---

ceoi1　seoi2　m4　maat3　zeoi2

吹水唔抹嘴

blowing water (chit-chatting) without wiping the mouth

吹牛不打草稿：形容人喜歡胡吹、
誇大其詞、信口開河
to talk big and nonsense ;
to be full of hot air

0538

口水多過茶
hau2 seoi2 do1 gwo3 caa4

more saliva than tea

形容人話多，總是説不完；
只會説不會做

to be garrulous or to chatter on and on ;
to be all talk and no action

0539

碌口水講過
loe1 hau2 seoi2 gong2 gwo3

**spit out the saliva
and say it again (differently)**

着人糾正剛才不吉利的説話，
吐口水重新説過合宜的話

to tell someone to take back
the words to avert bad luck from
what has just been said ; touch wood

0540

執人口水溦
zap1 jan4 hau2 seoi2 mei1

picking up others' saliva dribble

拾人涕唾，拾人牙慧，
學舌，人云亦云

to talk like a parrot and repeat what one has
heard ; to pass off words of others as one's own
without adding in any original ideas ; to follow
the crowd and say what everybody says

0541

隨口噏當秘笈
ceoi4 hau2 ngap1 dong3 bei3 kap1

**casually saying something and
take it as a secret manuscript**

胡謅亂説就當作大道理；
未經考證就當成事實般説出來

to make whimsical statements as if there is
truth in it ; to blabber as if speaking verified facts

0542

wu1 aa1 hau2
烏鴉口
the crow's beak

臭嘴巴，專說不中聽的話；
某人一說不吉利的話就應驗
to criticize someone for making displeasing
or inauspicious remarks ; a jinx whose
ominous comments often come true

0543

si1 zi2 hoi1 daai6 hau2
獅子開大口
the lion opens its mouth wide

開天殺價：在討價還價時開出
一個離譜得不能接受的價錢
highway / daylight robbery ;
to put the bite on someone in a bargain

0544

gun1 zi6 loeng5 go3 hau2
官字兩個口
**the chinese character for "government
official" got two mouths (in it)**

嘲諷官員權力大而獨斷專行，
歪理也可說成道理，百姓無從爭辯
you can't fight the City Hall - to criticize the government
officials for having too much power and resorting to
chicanery, overwhelming the will of the people

0545

sei3 maan6 gam2 hau2
四萬咁口
**(mahjong tile) forty
-thousand-like mouth**

形容人笑容可掬、露齒而笑
to be all smiles,
to have a broad grin

0546

紙紮下巴 > 口輕輕

zi2 zaat3 haa6 paa4　hau2 heng1 heng1

paper made chin > the mouth is light

輕易作出承諾；説話不負責任，輕率隨便
to make promise lightly ; to talk glibly about something

0547

精人出口，笨人出手

zeng1 jan4 ceot1 hau2　ban6 jan4 ceot1 sau2

a wise man uses mouth, a stupid man uses hands

嘲諷笨人被聰明人教唆或煽動做事，
終由笨人承擔後果，聰明人則坐享其成
to describe a satirical situation in which a clever person abets a fool to carry out
actions of his intention in a way that the fool takes all the associated responsibilities,
while the clever person simply enjoys the fruits of the fool's labour

0548

saam1　hau2　luk6　min6

三口六面
three mouths six faces

當面説清楚
to talk face-to-face to clarify things
or make things clear

0549

---

hak1　hau2　hak1　min6

黑口黑面
black mouth black face

形容人板起臉或一臉不悦的樣子
to pull a long face ; to be ill-humoured ;
to wear a scowl on one's face

0550

---

fu2　gwaa1　gon1　gam2　ge3　min6　hau2

苦瓜乾咁嘅面口
dried-bitter-gourd-like face and mouth

形容人愁眉苦臉
a sullen and sad face ;
to look miserable

0551

---

hau2　faa1　faa1

口花花
mouth flower flower

男人對女人説話輕佻
to describe a man who
talks glibly and frivolously
when flirting with women

0552

hau2 song2 ho4 baau1 nap6
口爽荷包溎
mouth is fresh (quick) but the wallet is sticky (tenacious)

嘴上疏爽，實質為人吝嗇，不肯掏錢；
引申指某人大方答應，卻沒有誠意做實事
to claim oneself to be generous but he is in fact a
miser ; to describe someone who pays lip service
to something without any intention of working on it

0553

sei2 zing6 baa2 hau2
死剩把口
all dead but being left with only a mouth

形容人強辯，嘴巴上從不服輸；
光說不做
to describe a person who never
yields to anyone in an argument ;
to be all talk and no action

0554

mou5 ji5 caa4 wu4 ／ dak1 baa2 hau2
冇耳茶壺＞得把口
earless teapot > having just a mouth

只說不做；
形容人說得頭頭是道，自己卻做不到
to pay lip service ; to describe someone as an armchair strategist
who likes to talk big but never really knows how to carry out a plan

0555

teeth.jpg

ngaa4 ci2 jan3
牙齒印
teeth mark

跟某人有過節或仇怨
to hold a grudge against someone ;
an old score that is yet to settle

0556

gai1 bei2 daa2 jan4 ngaa4 gaau3 jyun5
雞髀打人牙骹軟
**a chicken thigh beats
a man's teeth (and) jaw soft**

給人一些好處，對方自然就會答應你的要求
you can catch more flies with honey than with vinegar
– an offer of benefit is the best way of persuasion

0557

ngaa4 ci2 dong3 gam1 sai2
牙齒當金使
teeth are used as gold

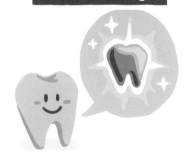

一諾千金：指人重承諾、言而有信。
在粵語中「口齒」是指信用
to be as good as one's words ; to keep one's
promise, as 「口齒」(mouth and teeth)
means one's credibility in Cantonese

0558

sat6 sik6 mou5 ci1 ngaa4
實食冇黐牙
**certainly can eat without
(anything) sticking to the teeth**

對於某事甚有把握，
肯定沒有問題
to be practically certain of something ;
to have something in the bag

0559

nose.jpg

daai6　bei6
大鼻
big nose

即「大牌」：
形容人態度囂張、
高傲有架子
a poser ; a big head ;
to be cocky

0560

baak6　bei6　go1
白鼻哥
white nose

源於戲曲中丑角的俗稱，多是湊熱鬧的
陪襯角色，現比喻到處拈花惹草（但總失敗）
的庸碌之輩；或指考試落第的無能之人
a failed womanizer ; a person who fails in exams,
as it originates from the amusing and silly "Clown" role
in Chinese operas who has white paint on his nose

0561

duk1　ngaan5　duk1　bei6
篤眼篤鼻
pricking eyes pricking nose

形容某人或事物很討厭，
怎樣看都不順眼
a pain in the arse ;
an irritant or annoyance

0562

hau2　tung4　bei6　aau3
口同鼻拗
the mouth and nose quarrel

難以達成共識或結論的無謂爭執；
爭論的各方都未能提供實質證明
a meaningless and inconclusive argument ;
neither side of the dispute can prove its
version of the same fact

0563

haak3 dou3 bei6 go1 lung1 dou1 mou5 juk6

嚇到鼻哥窿都冇肉

so scared that even the nostrils lost flesh

以幽默或自嘲手法形容人被嚇壞了，
十分驚恐
to be scared stiff ;
to quake in one's boots

0564

---

tung4 jat1 go3 bei6 lung1 ceot1 hei3

同一個鼻窿出氣

exhaling through the same nostril

以貶損的語氣指稱其他人站在同一陣線
或採取一致的觀點和主張（而該立場與自己對立）
a derogatory way to say that some parties, which are
in conflict with oneself, sing the same tune

0565

bei6 go1 lung1 daam1 ze1　　bei6 mou4　　ho2 bei6

鼻哥窿擔遮 > 鼻毛(避無)可避

nostrils holding an umbrella
> nose hair can take shelter (from the rain)

想逃避卻無處可逃，即無法避免的
to describe something as inevitable or inexorable,
as the saying is a wordplay with two pairs of homophones:
「鼻」(nose) and 「避」(avoid / evade / hide from) ,
「毛」(hair) and 「無」(not)

0566

---

bin2 bei6 go1 daai3 ngaan5 geng2　　nei5 gan2 keoi5 m4 gan2

扁鼻哥戴眼鏡 > 你緊佢唔緊

flat nose wearing glasses
> yours is tight, his is not tight (you care but he doesn't)

你認為應該着緊的事，對方卻顯得毫不在乎
what someone regards as important is not taken seriously
by another person involved, as 「緊」(tight) in Cantonese
also means to care and be worried about something

0567

head.jpg

洗濕個頭

sai2 sap1 go3 tau4

washed and wetted the head (hair)

開弓沒有回頭箭：事情已經開了頭，
只能硬着頭皮做下去，不能反悔了
once you have started something,
there's no turning back

0568

險過剃頭

him2 gwo3 tai3 tau4

more dangerous than shaving the head

險象環生而僥倖脫險
a close shave or a close call

0569

爭崩頭

zaang1 bang1 tau4

compete broken head

競爭非常激烈
fierce rivalry ;
intense and keen competition

0570

舂個頭埋去

zung1 go3 tau4 maai4 heoi3

pound the head in it

莽撞地參與一件事，
或盲目地投入一段感情之中
to rush headlong into something
or an unsuitable relationship

0571

ngok6 jyu4 tau4 lou5 can3 dai2
鱷魚頭老襯底
crocodile head
(but) an old dupe underneath

gun1 jam1 tau4 sou2 baa2 goek3
觀音頭掃把腳
Guanyin's head (but) broom's leg

外表看來很兇惡、精明，
骨子裏其實易哄易騙
a person who looks vicious is in fact
a gudgeon who is easily wheedled

比喻人上半身打扮端莊得體，
下半身卻草草了事，極不合襯；
或指某事虎頭蛇尾
to describe someone who dresses up
the upper body but not the lower body ;
to start off with a bang
but end up with a whimper

0572

0573

54

pai1　go3　tau4　lok6　lai4　bei2　nei5　dong3　dang3　co5

批個頭落嚟俾你當櫈坐

cut my head off and let you sit on it like a stool

對自己的估計或諾言很有信心，
甚至可用自己的頭（性命）來打賭
an exaggerated expression one uses to show his confidence in his prediction
or keeping his promise, that he can even bet his head (life) on it

0574

---

jau5　tau4　faat3　bin1　go3　soeng2　zou6　laat3　lei1

有頭髮邊個想做癩痢

(if) having hair, who wants to have favid?

所做的事乃為勢所迫、身不由己
to be forced to do something willy-nilly ;
to express helplessly that one cannot choose one's own path in life

0575

juk1　sau2
郁手
moving hands

動手打人，動武
to rough up or to strike someone ;
to start a fight

0576

sai2　waang4　sau2
使橫手
use the horizontal hand

使用不正當或不光彩的手段
to use dirty,
disreputable or illegal means

0577

saam1　zek3　sau2
三隻手
three hands

偷東西的扒手
a pickpocket

0578

daan6　gung1　sau2
彈弓手
coil spring hand

猜拳時違規的小把戲，即玩家臨時改變
手勢；引申指反覆無常的臨時改動
to play a trick in hand games such as morra
or rock-paper-scissors, like changing the throw
at the last moment ; to act inconsistently or
capriciously in the course of implementation

0579

Sau2 ting4 hau2 ting4
手停口停
hands stop (then) mouth stops

一不幹活便沒收入，以至三餐不繼，
或指沒有固定收入或底薪的工作
to live hand to mouth ;
to work for a job that doesn't offer a basic salary

0580

coeng1 Sau2
槍手
gun hand (gunman)

代筆作家、影子寫手，
或頂替別人做功課或考試的人
a gunner ; a ghostwriter or someone
who passes himself off as a candidate to
take an exam for another person

0581

sap6 zek3 Sau2 zi2 jau5 coeng4 dyun2
十隻手指有長短
(speaking of) the ten fingers there are long and short (ones)

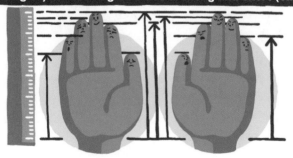

人人各有自己的強項與弱點，
多比喻同出的子女或同一班學生各有不同
everyone has his own strengths and weaknesses, mostly referring
to comparison among siblings or students in the same class

0582

Sau2 baan2 jau6 hai6 juk6　Sau2 bui3 jau6 hai6 juk6

手板又係肉，手背又係肉

the palm is flesh, the back of the hand is also flesh

形容人左右為難，兩邊都是相熟的人，不知幫誰好
one is caught in the middle or finds it difficult to maintain
an impartial position as he has a close relationship
with both parties that he has been sandwiched between

0583

Sau2　zi2　aau5　ceot1　m4　aau5　jap6

手指拗出唔拗入

fingers bending outwards (but) not bending inwards

吃裏扒外：幫外人不幫自己人
to describe someone who helps the competitors or takes the opponents' side
while he is expected to show support to his own team or family

0584

Sau2 gan2
手緊
hands (are) tight

缺錢用，手頭周轉不靈
to be cash-strapped or short of cash ;
to be out at the elbows

0585

Sau2 zi2 laa3 so1
手指罅疏
the gaps between fingers (are) wide

形容人存不下錢，花錢大手大腳
to describe someone as spending money
like water, being unable to save money

0586

jat1 zek3 Sau2 zoeng2 paak3 m4 hoeng2
一隻手掌拍唔響
one palm's clap cannot make a sound

糾紛或感情關係都不是單獨一方可以挑起的，
雙方必然都有責任
it takes two to make a quarrel ; it takes two to tango

0587

laang5 Sau2 zap1 go3 jit6 zin1 deoi1

冷手執個熱煎堆

cold hand picking up a hot sesame ball

不須努力就撿到意外的便宜
without any effort one receives
an unexpected gain or opportunity by luck

0588

---

fei1 m4 ceot1 ngo5 Sau2 zi2 laa3

飛唔出我手指罅

(one) cannot fly away from (slip through) my fingers

指另一方沒能逃離自己的掌控
to be assured that someone else
can hardly escape from one's control

0589

leg.jpg

gwo3　ho4　sap1　goek3
過河濕腳
crossing river wet (one's) legs

只要有錢財或交易經手，
某人必從中刮取若干
to take a cut or commission from a
business deal ; to get some benefit from
anything that comes one's way
0590

sai2　goek3　m4　maat3　goek3
洗腳唔抹腳
washing the feet but not drying the feet

揮霍金錢：廣東人以水喻錢財，洗完腳
任水隨處滴，即解作毫不吝嗇地花錢
a spendthrift ; to criticize someone for playing
ducks and drakes with his money, as "water"
symbolizes "money" in Cantonese, so the water
dripped metaphorically means the money squandered
0591

gwan2　seoi2　luk6　goek3
滾水淥腳
boiling water over feet

因腳被沸水燙到而不停跳動，
比喻人慌忙走動，
或來去匆匆而不作停留
to be in a great hurry ;
to be flustered and run around
0592

lam4　gap1　pou5　fat6　goek3
臨急抱佛腳
in emergency hug the Buddha's leg

平時無準備，事急才倉促張羅或求助；
現多指學生在最後關頭才準備考試
to seek help or make hasty preparation at
the last moment ; to cram for one's exams
0593

laai1 jan4 kwan4 kam2 zi6 gei2 goek3

拉人裙搣自己腳

pull other's dress over one's own legs

借別人之物令自己獲得好處，或叨別人
的光，借用別人的聲望來抬高自己
to exploit the interest of others so as to gain an
advantage for oneself ; to bask in reflected glory

0594

---

daa2 bai1 goek3 m4 sai2 jau1

打跛腳唔使憂

even if one broke his leg and went lame, there is no need to worry

因獲得橫財或找到靠山而得以
過富裕的生活，從此不愁衣食
one is able to lead a wealthy, carefree life
upon receiving a windfall or financial backing

0595

---

aak1 ngo5 sat1 tau4 go1 m4 sik6 laat6 ziu1 zoeng3

呃我膝頭哥唔食辣椒醬

(don't you) cheat my knees, they wouldn't eat chili sauce

指責人説話不可信：
別把我當傻瓜，這麼簡單顯淺的道理還拿來騙我？
you lie like a cheap Thai watch
– to express disbelief in someone's words

0596

64

haang4 wan6 haang4 dou3 lok6 goek3 zi2 mei1

行運行到落腳趾尾

to be so lucky that even the little toe is in luck

非常幸運或僥倖
to be very lucky indeed

0597

tau4 tung3 ji1 tau4 goek3 tung3 ji1 goek3

頭痛醫頭，腳痛醫腳

(having) headache cure the head, (having) foot ache cure the foot

只醫治疼痛的部位而不追究病根：
諷刺人治標不治本，只會被動地應付問題
to cure the symptoms, not the disease ; to tackle the presenting problem
without an intention to come up with an ultimate solution dealing with the core issue

0598

hair.jpg

aa3 mou4
阿毛
ah hair

應為「阿嬤」，老婆婆的
俗稱，源自台山話「阿母」
a common term for "granny",
which originates from Taishanese

0599

daam2 saang1 mou4
膽生毛
gallbladder grows hair

形容人大膽，卻不免莽撞、不分輕重：
古人認為膽主勇斷，毛則象徵野蠻、
沒智慧的野人
to be audacious and dauntless but somehow
reckless (like a hairy barbarian) - in traditional
Chinese belief the gallbladder masters one's bravery

0600

jau5 mou4 jau5 jik6
有毛有翼
**having feathers
having wings**

父母用於譏誚兒女羽翼已成，
不屑倚靠自己，因此也不再聽教了
an idiom mainly used by parents to satirize
their teenage children for being rebellious,
as they are "fully fledged" to fly the nest

0601

sung1 mou4 sung1 jik6
鬆毛鬆翼
**loosening feathers
loosening wings**

自滿、洋洋得意的樣子
to be complacent about
one's own achivement ;
to be proud and self-satisfied

0602

蟲 bug P.92

雀 bird P.84

龍 dragon P.70

蛙 frog P.88

坊劇粵鳳龍

狼 wolf P.82

羊 sheep P.80

猴 monkey P.76

dragon.jpg

jan4 lung4
人龍
people dragon

排隊隊伍
a long queue of people

0603

lyun6 lung4
亂龍
messy dragon

形容事物亂七八糟、雜亂無章；
對事情感到很困惑、混淆
to describe something as utterly messy,
chaotic or disorderly ;
to be confused about something

0604

ding2 lung2
頂龍
top dragon

極其量、最盡；有指「龍」的本字
為「櫳」，指西關大屋的趟櫳門，
「頂櫳」是指人多得擠出門口了
to have reached a place's
maximum capacity ; at most

0605

gwo3 lung4
過龍
(pass) over a dragon

泛指做過了頭或做多了，「坐過龍」是指
乘車坐過了站；「眼大睇過龍」即看漏了
眼前明顯的事物；「瞓過龍」則指睡過頭
to overdo things ; it can be used in other phrases
to mean having missed the stop, having
overlooked something or having overslept

0606

baai2 wu1 lung2
擺烏龍
place a black dragon

搞了糊塗或出差錯
to goof or to blunder ;
to make inadvertent errors

0607

duk6 ngaan5 lung4
獨眼龍
single eye dragon

一目失明的人
a cyclops, one-eyed person ;
a person who is blind in one eye

0608

lung4 jau2
龍友
dragon buddies

「龍」是指「沙龍」,
龍友即業餘攝影愛好者
an amateur photography enthusiast,
as the word "lung4" originates from the
transliteration of "Salon Photography"

0609

daa2 lung4 tung1
打龍通
break through dragon

有指是「打聾通」,原指打麻將時
其中二人打眼色串通,令別人出沖;
後引申指串謀的行為
it originates from collusion in mahjong games in
which two players send signal to each other to make
other players lose ; now it means conspiracy to cheat

0610

ng5 zaau2 gam1 lung4
五爪金龍
five-clawed golden dragon

戲稱人不用餐具，
直接用五隻手指抓東西吃
to laugh at people who grab food
and eat with bare hands

0611

jat1 tiu4 lung4
一條龍
one dragon

一站式服務；
直屬或聯繫學校制度
one-stop services ;
through-train schools

0612

m4 hai6 maang5 lung4 m4 gwo3 gong1
唔係猛龍唔過江
(if it were) not a fierce dragon it would not cross the river

出來闖蕩的都是有本事、實力雄厚的人，不能小覷
a competent challenger from a
far-off land is not to be underestimated

0613

jat1　si3　bin6　zi1　lung4　jyu5　fung6

一試便知龍與鳳

as soon as you try you know if it is dragon or phoenix

不必再花心思猜度，大可測試或驗證一下
就知道事物或事情實際是如何
the proof of the pudding is in the eating
– a test can reveal the truth

0614

---

haang4　wan6　jat1　tiu4　lung4　　seoi1　wan6　jat1　tiu4　cung4

行運一條龍，衰運一條蟲

good luck, a dragon ; bad luck, a worm

比喻人運氣好時事事順境，
運氣差時則事多阻滯、窮途潦倒，境況可有天淵之別
everything falls into place when one's star is rising,
or everything sucks when one is down on his luck

0615

gwat6 mei5 lung2 · gaau2 fung1 gaau2 jyu5
掘尾龍 〉攪風攪雨

blunt-tailed dragon > stirring up wind and rain

每當天氣驟變，風雨交加，便會説是斷了尾巴的龍來掃墓了：
比喻愛製造麻煩、興風作浪的人
a troublemaker

0616

---

sik6 zo2 cou2 lung2 · hou2 coeng3 hau2
食咗草龍 〉好唱口

have eaten grass dragon (grass lizard) > a good singing mouth

比喻人心情好，會情不自禁地哼起歌來，
像籠鳥吃了草龍（南草蜥）後，唱歌也特別開朗而嘹亮
to tease someone who happily hums, wondering why he is in such a good mood

0617

monkey.jpg

maa5 lau1 zing1
馬騮精
monkey elf

頑皮的小孩
an active, mischievous child

0618

lat1 sing2 maa5 lau1
甩繩馬騮
loose string monkey

到處亂闖的頑皮小孩，
像脫了繩子束縛的猴子
a naughty kid who breaks away
from his guardians

0619

hau4 kam4
猴擒
monkey catches

同「猴急」：
形容焦急、急不及待的樣子；
個性急進
to be as impatient as a monkey
– to be antsy or straining at the leash

0620

maa5 lau1 zap1 gat1
馬騮執桔
monkey picks up a calamondin

因意外收獲而歡喜若狂
someone is thrilled by an unexpected gain,
as if he has discovered buried treasure

0621

zou6 maa5 lau1 hei3
做馬騮戲
do a monkey play

形容人做事徒具形式、裝模作樣；
賣弄花巧，只做門面工夫；
引申意思為一場鬧劇
to put on an act to win someone's favour
or sympathy ; to stage a farce

0622

maa5 lau1 si2 fat1
馬騮屎窟
monkey's butt

形容女人化妝時胭脂用太多，
如猴子屁股一樣紅
a woman's face is red like a monkey's butt
when she wears too much rouge

0623

hung4 hung4 luk6 luk6　maa5 lau1 ji1 fuk6
紅紅綠綠，馬騮衣服
red red green green, monkey's clothes

嘲諷人不懂配搭衣服，只會標奇立異，結果弄巧反拙
to tease someone about wearing an outfit of mismatched wild colours

0624

maa5 lau1 sing1 gun1　　m4 hai6 jan4 gam2 ban2

馬騮升官 〉唔係人咁品

monkey gets promoted as a government official > not like a human

令人難以招架，多形容某人不通人性或脾氣乖僻；
不是省油的燈：不好惹、難搞的人物
a heartless and wacky person who is not easy to cope with ;
a difficult person to deal with

0625

---

seoi2 zam3 maa5 lau1　　ngaan5 maak3 maak3

水浸馬騮 〉眼擘擘

water swamps the monkey > eyes open wide

形容人驚慌失措時，瞪大雙眼乾着急
to be panic-stricken

0626

sheep.jpg

joeng4 gu2
羊牯
sacrificial lamb

待宰以作祭祀的羔羊：
比喻被人騙取利益的外行人
a greenhorn or a patsy ;
an innocent layman who is easily duped

0627

min4 joeng2 zai2
綿羊仔
little lamb

「速克達」踏板式輕便電單車
scooter

0628

joeng4 mou4 ceot1 zi6 joeng4 san1 soeng6
羊毛出自羊身上
the fleece comes from the sheep's body

比喻所獲得的利益實際是來自自己本身的付出
all charges are shifted to customers,
there's no such thing as a free lunch

0629

wolf.jpg

long4 toi1
狼胎
wolf's fetus

形容人做事兇狠、不要命，
或過分進取而不顧後果
to be too aggressive ; to be malignant,
disregarding all possible consequences

0630

long4 Sam1 gau2 fai3
狼心狗肺
wolf's heart, dog's lung

像狼和狗一樣心腸狠毒、忘恩負義
to be as cruel as a wolf
and as savage as a cur
– to be wicked, unscrupulous and ungrateful

0631

sik1 long4
色狼
coloured wolf

非禮甚至性侵犯女性的男人
a sexual predator

0632

long4 gwo3 waa4 sau3 zek3 gau2
狼過華秀隻狗
more (wolflike) vicious than Wah Sau's dog

傳說華秀是個橫蠻的惡霸，養了幾頭惡犬，
經常咬傷人；形容某人做事異常心狠手辣
to describe someone to be more malignant than anyone

0633

bird.jpg

man4　zoek2

文雀
sparrow

文雀喜偷吃農作物，礙於其細小而全身
黃褐色，農民難以發現；現借喻扒手
to refer to pickpockets who are like sparrows
stealing crops in the field without being noticed

0634

gam1　si1　zoek2

金絲雀
canary

女子打扮得花姿招展來吸引異性；或指
被富豪包養，金屋藏嬌而不用工作的女子
a woman who dolls herself up to attract men ;
a sugar baby who lives in a luxurious house
and doesn't have to work for a living

0635

am1　ceon1

鵪鶉
quail

膽小怕事，易受驚的
a timid or chicken-hearted person ;
to quail at someone or something

0636

hoi1　lung4　zoek2

開籠雀
a bird set free from an open cage

形容人活潑多話，像被困的鳥兒突然
獲得釋放，無拘無束地唱歌一樣
to babble on like a bird that is singing in
an unbridled way when it is set free from a cage

0637

tong1 baak6 hok2
劏白鶴

slaughter a white crane

酒後嘔吐：「湯白喝」的諧音，
現多簡稱「劏」
to throw up after drinking alcohol,
as the phrase is a wordplay implying that
"the wine was vainly drunk"

0638

tong4 bin1 hok2
塘邊鶴

cranes standing by the pond

胡亂插嘴或議論，
但從不參與的旁觀者
a bystander or kibitzer who likes
to give advice or criticism

0639

ngo4 gung1 hau4
鵝公喉

gander's voice box

形容一些女性低沉沙啞的聲線
a woman's low and husky voice

0640

daa2 go3 baak6 gaap3 zyun3
打個白鴿轉

take a pigeon turn

到附近走走，兜一圈又回來；
或形容車輛失控而原地轉圈
to roam around and pay a short visit to and
from a place ; to describe a vehicle that loses
control and spins around

0641

hak1 baak6 tin1 ngo4　　jat6 ngo4　　je6 ngo4
黑白天鵝＞日鵝(哦) 夜鵝(哦)

black swan and white swan > day swan and night swan

沒日沒夜、整天在嘮叨着某人：除了「鵝」字是「哦」的諧音字，
「天」字亦一語雙關，解「天鵝」、「白天」和「黑夜」

to nag someone day and night, as 「鵝」(swan) also sounds like "chatter" in Cantonese,
and the word 「天」(sky) is a pun used to indicate "swan", "daytime" and nighttime"

0642

---

wong4 pei2 syu6 liu1 go1　　m4 suk6 m4 sik6
黃皮樹鷯哥＞唔熟唔食

hill myna on a wampee tree > they never eat unripe fruits

專佔熟人的便宜，只去欺騙熟悉的朋友

to describe someone who cheats or takes advantage of nobody but his close friends,
as 「熟」(ripe) also means "to be close or familiar with a friend" in Cantonese

0643

frog.jpg

蛤乸衣

gaap3　naa2　ji1

toad's outfit

連衫褲工作服

boilersuit,
dungarees

0644

---

bin1　jau5　　gam3　daai6　zek3　gaap3　naa2　ceoi4　gaai1　tiu3

（邊有）咁大隻蛤乸隨街跳

what a big toad hopping around the street

「哪會有這麼大的好處？」好得令人難以置信

to be surprised by a deal which is too good to be true

0645

ziu3　tin4　gai1

照田雞

shine (the flashlight) on a frog

田雞怕光，被照着了就會一動不動
任人抓：現指故意用燈照着夜間
在戶外親熱的情侶

to play a prank on couples who make out in
public at night by putting a spotlight on them

0646

tin4　gai1　dung1　　gaap3　dung1

田雞東 〉蛤東

frog proprietor > toad proprietor

蛤即田雞，蛤東是「夾東」的諧音，意即夾
錢作東：吃飯結帳大夥兒一同分攤、AA制

to split the bill ; to go dutch, as 「蛤」(toad)
and 「夾」(share, chip in) are homophones
in Cantonese

0647

lung4　min2　tin4　gai1　maan6　zaau2　haai5

籠面田雞慢爪蟹

a frog on top of the cage, a slowly crawling crab

在籠子表面也不懂得逃走的田雞，以及走得很慢的蟹，
都是將死的模樣，比喻劣質貨

a lemon, goods of low quality – a frog that doesn't escape when the cage is
open and a crab that crawls slowly mean that they are functional impaired
or even dying, proving that they are not fresh enough to eat

0648

tin4　gai1　gwo3　ho4　　gok3　jau5　gok3　jaan3

田雞過河 > 各有各蹍

frogs crossing the river > each hopping in its own way

危難的時候各顧各逃離四散；各奔前路

to go separate ways ;
to go one's own way in critical moments

0649

---

laai3　haa1　mou1　soeng2　sik6　tin1　ngo4　juk6

癩蝦蟆想食天鵝肉

a toad wishes to eat swan meat

比喻人沒有自知之明，不自量力，妄想謀取不可能到手的東西；
追求條件比自己好得多的對象

to crave for what one is not worthy of ; to woo someone who is out of one's league

0650

bug.jpg

zam1　baan2　ngai5

砧板蟻

ants on the chopping board

為食鬼：不知死活地貪吃的人
a glutton
(who is like ants finding food at all costs)

0651

jat1　san1　ngai5

一身蟻

whole body full of ants

惹來了一身麻煩
to be in hot water ;
to be in serious trouble up to one's neck

0652

ngai5　laan1　gam2

蟻躝咁

crawl like ants

比喻人走路太慢
to describe someone walking
or something moving terribly slowly

0653

ngai5　do1　lau1　sei2　zoeng6

蟻多摟死象

**a large number of ants can kill an
elephant by crawling all over its body**

比喻弱者人多而齊心，可以戰勝強者
there is strength in numbers ;
to overcome a powerful opponent by sheer number

0654

paak3 wu1 jing1
拍烏蠅
swat a fly

形容生意冷清，商店沒人光顧，
店員空閒得在拍烏蠅
business is deplorably dull with very few
customers, as the shop assistants have
nothing to do but to swat flies

0655

daa2 wu1 jing1
打烏蠅
hit a fly

在重大案件中只捉拿小官員，
卻放過犯事的大官員
to arrest the petty officials only and let off
the senior officials involved in a major crime

0656

maang4 tau4 wu1 jing1　lyun6 zung1 lyun6 zong6
盲頭烏蠅 〉亂舂亂撞
blind-headed flies > fly around blindly

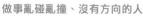

做事亂碰亂撞、沒有方向的人
to be like a bull in a china shop ;
to run around like a headless chicken

0657

sai3 man1 zai2
細蚊仔
little mosquito boy

小孩子
kids

0658

---

man1 dou1 fan3
蚊都瞓
even the mosquito sleeps

等得蚊子也睡了：恐怕太遲了
to be way too late

0659

---

man1 bei2 tung4 ngau4 bei2
蚊髀同牛髀
mosquito's thigh Vs. cow's thigh

小巫見大巫：二者有天淵之別，不能相比
a markedly huge difference between
two things to an extent that they are
almost completely incomparable

0660

---

paau2 maa5 se6 man1 sou1
跑馬射蚊鬚
**ride a horse and shoot at
a mosquito's whiskers**

比喻毫無把握，機會十分渺茫
chances are slim, no guarantee of success

0661

應聲蟲
jing3 sing1 cung4

echo bug

唯唯諾諾、只會附和別人的人
a yes-man, an echo

0662

地頭蟲
dei6 tau4 cung4

local bug

熟習環境的本地人；
「猛虎不及地頭蟲」，意謂再強的外來者
也壓不住當地的勢力
local people know the place the best that the
powerful incomers can hardly afford to neglect

0663

垃圾蟲
laap6 saap3 cung4

litterbug

隨地亂拋垃圾的人
a litterer

0664

蛀書蟲
zyu3 syu1 cung4

bookworm

喜愛讀書者；
書呆子：一心讀書不問窗外事的人
a bookworm, a swot

0665

haam4 cung4
鹹 蟲
salty worm

色鬼：廣東話中「鹹濕」
是好色的意思，
「鹹蟲」即急色之人
a lascivious person, a lecher

0666

zaam2 goek3 zi2 bei6 saa1 cung2
斬腳趾避沙蟲
chop off the toes to avoid sandworms

有指「沙蟲」本義為腳氣，古人誤以為足癬
乃沙蟲蛀蝕所致。斬腳趾以防足癬或沙蟲，即為
避小害而作出過大犧牲的愚蠢行為；因噎廢食
to make big sacrifice to avoid minor troubles

0667

bai1 goek3 liu1 go1 zi6 jau5 fei1 loi4 maang5
跛腳鷯哥自有飛來蜢
a lame hill myna will still have a fly-in grasshopper

再不濟的人也會有送上門的好運氣；
引申含義是即使你身處困境，仍有翻身的機遇
one may still experience unexpected luck in the midst of difficulties ;
things will sort themselves out ; God will provide

0668

fei1 tin1 kam4 lou2
飛天蠄蟧
flying spider

爬外牆潛入屋爆竊的飛賊
a cat burglar who enters and leaves
a flat by climbing up walls

0669

wong4 fung1 jiu1 gaat6 zaat2 tou5
黃蜂腰甲由肚
hornet's waist, cockroach's belly

比喻女性身材美好，如黃蜂纖細的腰，
與蟑螂平坦光滑的小腹
to describe a woman who has a great figure,
with her waist as slim as hornets' and belly
as flat as cockroaches'

0670

baak3 zuk1 gom3 do1 zaau2
百足咁多爪
as many claws as a centipede

形容人身兼多職，或活躍於不同
界別、人面廣；興趣廣泛
to wear more than one hat – a person who is
involved in many businesses and sectors ;
to have a wide range of interests

0671

mou5 sat1 wan2 sat1 aau1
冇蝨搵蝨抓
**(when there is) no lice, one still
looks for lice for scratching**

沒事找事，自找麻煩
to stir up a hornet's nest
– to go looking for trouble

0672

hou2 mei4 hou2 maau6 saang1 saa1 sat1

好眉好貌生沙蝨

(though with) good eyebrows and good looking one breeds sand lice

「沙蝨」實指番薯上的小黑洞，煮熟後有難聞的氣味：
比喻人長得眉清目秀，卻擁有壞心腸
a person who looks nice on the outside is actually rotten inside,
as "sand lice" are the tiny black holes in sweet potatoes that get stinky after being cooked

0673

---

jat1 mat6 zi6 jat1 mat6 no6 mai5 zi6 muk6 sat1

一物治一物，糯米治木蝨

there is always one thing to conquer another,
glutinous rice can kill wood lice (bedbug)

萬物相生相剋，一種東西一定有別的東西可以克制它
everything has its vanquisher
– there is an inter-inhibiting relation among things in the world

0674

鑊
wok
P.120

食物
food
P.102

煲
pot
P.124

刀
knife
P.114

田
field
P.130

和尚
monk
P.127

屎
faeces
P.136

泥沙
mud & sand
P.132

灶
stove
P.118

碗
bowl
P.112

food.jpg

lo4 dai2 caang2
籮底橙
oranges at the bottom of basket

剩下沒人要的東西；次貨；
成績最差的學生；嫁不出去的女人
leftovers or broken goods ; the worst student with
the poorest performance ; spinsters

0675

ngau4 juk6 gon1
牛肉乾
beef jerky

交通警發出的告票
（定額罰款通知書）
parking tickets (fixed penalty notices)
issued by traffic wardens

0676

baau1 wan4 tan1
包雲吞
wrap wontons

不停用紙巾包起鼻涕
to continuously blow the runny nose
and fold up the snot in tissue papers

0677

gam1 bo1 lo1
金菠蘿
gold pineapple

源自古代盛美酒的金製酒器「金叵羅」，
引申形容珍貴的事物或人，
今尤指受寵的寶貝子女或孫兒
to mainly refer to one's darling children or grand-
children – the idiom originates from the precious
golden wine cup in ancient times

0678

茶樓例湯 〉整定
caa4 lau4 lai6 tong1   zing2 ding6

restaurant's soup of the day > prepared in advance

某些事情早已被命運注定
to admit that one's misfortune is fated and reconcile
oneself to one's lot, as in Cantonese「整定」also
means that something is predetermined

0679

頭啖湯
tou4 daam6 tong1

the first sip of the soup

捷足先登、把握先機，
比別人先得到的好處
the early bird gets the worm
– to be the first to take the most
advantage of something

0680

女人湯丸
neoi5 jan2 tong1 jyun2

woman's soup ball (glutinous rice ball)

深得女性喜愛、
在女人堆中打滾的男性
a ladies' man
– a man who is popular among women
and enjoys their company

0681

唔湯唔水
m4 tong1 m4 seoi2

neither soup nor water

弄得不三不四的；做事半途而廢，
弄得不像話，無法收場
neither fish nor fowl ; to be perfunctory and
give up halfway, making a mess of things

0682

運桔

wan6 gat1

transport the calamondins

看似來光顧或幫忙，誰知只是瞎弄而浪費自己
時間：新年時把年桔運往商舖兜售，影響別人做
生意；另有指是從前有人到餐廳喝過附送的
吉水（湯水）後便溜掉，「混口吉水喝」而不光顧

to visit a shop or a person without any particular purpose,
wasting people's time ; to raise someone's expectation
but then disappoint him

0683

着到隻糉咁

zoek3 dou3 zek3 zung2 gam2

**dress like a
sticky rice dumpling**

穿了一身厚重的衣服，
像糉子一樣

to wrap oneself up in heavy clothes

0684

上面蒸鬆糕，下面賣涼粉

soeng6 min6 zing1 sung1 gou1　haa6 min6 maai6 loeng4 fan2

steaming sponge cake on top, selling cool powder (grass jelly) below

上身衣服穿得厚厚的，密實得像在蒸鬆糕，
下身卻只穿短褲或短裙，很清涼的樣子

to describe someone who wears heavy top or coat but mini skirts or shorts

0685

hoi2　Sin1　gaa3
海鮮價
seafood price

像海鮮一樣跟隨時價發售：
浮動的價格
a current price that floats like the
"market price" on restaurant menus

0686

---

dim6　gwo3　luk1　ze3
掂過碌蔗
straighter than a sugar cane

非常順利、妥當：「掂」是雙關語，
有「直／豎」及「成功」之意
everything goes smoothly and favourably,
as「掂」also means perfectly alright and
successful in Cantonese

0687

---

bun2　dei6　goeng1
本地薑
local (-ly grown) ginger

本地人才
local talents

0688

---

gau3　goeng1
夠薑
enough ginger

形容人勇猛、膽子大，不畏強權
to have the guts and be daring,
not submitting to force

0689

man2 goeng1
瘟薑
badtempered ginger

暴躁、煩躁、容易動怒的人
a short-tempered, impatient person

0690

goeng1 jyu6 lou5 jyu6 laat6
薑愈老愈辣
the older the ginger, the spicier

人愈年長，經驗愈豐富，性格愈剛強
what an old man sees while sitting,
a young man cannot see while standing
— the older one grows, the more experienced
and capable one becomes

0691

gaau3 coi3 lou5 goeng1 saang1 coi3 zai2 › gaa3 co3 lou5 gung1 saang1 co3 zai2
芥菜老薑生菜仔›嫁錯老公生錯仔
**mustard, old ginger, little lettuce
> marrying the wrong husband, bearing the wrong son**

諧音歇後語，埋怨自己嫁錯郎，兒子又不孝順聽教
this two-part allegorical saying is a wordplay describing a woman's complaint
about marrying the wrong guy and having an unfilial and disobedient son

0692

loeng5 so1 ziu1
兩梳蕉
two bunches of bananas

去探訪親友但沒有預備禮物，
兩手空空，十指垂下像兩把香蕉
to visit someone without bringing anything,
for a pair of bare hands looks like bunches
of bananas

0693

hoeng1 ziu1 zai2
香蕉仔
banana boy

「黃皮白心」：指海外出生的華裔，有
黃種人的外表，內在卻是白人的文化
American-born or overseas Chinese
(i.e. yellow-skinned) who are westernized
(i.e.white-hearted)

0694

aa3 mau6 zing2 beng2　mou5 go2 joeng6 zing2 go2 joeng6
阿茂整餅 > 冇嗰樣整嗰樣
ah mau makes cakes > no such model, make such model

沒事找事做，多此一舉；
做出來的東西沒有實用價值，甚至弄糟原本的事情
to do something unnecessary ;
to have done something superfluous that ruined the original task or plan

0695

gwaa1　　　gwaa1 caai4　　gwaa1 lou5 can3

瓜 / 瓜柴 / 瓜老襯
melon / melon firewood / melon old fool

死亡

to be dead ; to kick the bucket ; to bite the dust

0696

---

tang4 nang3 gwaa1　gwaa1 nang3 tang4

藤揗瓜 瓜揗藤
vine tangles with the melon, melon tangles with the vine

事情或關係糾纏不清、難以分離

to describe things or relations to be closely
related and intertwined with one another,
to an extent that they are no longer separable

0697

dung1 gwaa1 dau6　fu6

冬瓜豆腐
winter melon and bean curd

舊時辦過喪事後，答謝親友的素席上會有
冬瓜、豆腐：引申指遭逢不測或死於非命

to refer to misfortune, accidental or violent death,
as winter melon and bean curd are served
in the banquet that is held in gratitude for
the visit of the relatives after a funeral

0698

mo2 zau2 bui1 dai2
摸酒杯底
touch the wine glasses' bottom

跟別人喝酒談心，坦誠溝通
to have a heart-to-heart talk

0699

gaa1 jim4 gaa1 cou3
加鹽加醋
add salt add vinegar

在敘事或轉述說話時誇大或渲染內容
to exaggerate or make up stories when
recounting an incident or repeating
what one was told

0700

si6 jau4 laau1 faan6   zing2 sik1 zing2 seoi2
豉油撈飯 > 整色整水
soy sauce stirred rice > make colour, make water

將醬油加在白飯上，只是調弄顏色：
裝樣子，刻意製造假象誤導別人
window dressing ; to put on airs and graces ;
to use little tricks to mislead people

0701

laau1　jau4　seoi2

撈 油 水

stir oil water

利用職權中飽私囊，或用不當的
手段從中獲利或得到好處
to abuse one's authority to line his
own pockets ; to gain profits or take
advantages by underhand means

0702

ding6　gwo3　toi4　jau4

定 過 抬 油

stabler than carrying oil (with a pole)

比用肩挑油還穩當：
鎮定自若，對事情有十足把握
to be perfectly calm and collected ;
to handle a task with absolute confidence

0703

gaak3　je6　jau4　zaa3　gwai2　　mou5　lei4　fo2　hei3

隔 夜 油 炸 鬼 ＞ 冇 厘 火 氣

(left) overnight chinese oil stick > no fire air (heat) at all

脾氣很好、不易發怒的人；
缺乏朝氣、太和善而無個性的人
a very good-tempered person who never gets angry ;
a person who lacks assertiveness or character

0704

bowl.jpg

ziu3 baan2 zyu2 wun2
照辦煮碗

follow the sample to cook another bowl

依樣畫葫蘆；照樣重複來一次
to copy mechanically from a model ;
to follow suit ; to consciously do
the exact same thing again

0705

bang1 hau2 jan4　gei6　bang1 hau2 wun2
崩口人忌崩口碗

a cleft-lipped person shuns using chipped bowls

當着矮人別説短話：提醒人説話時不要犯忌，
別觸及他人的弱點或傷處，以避影射之嫌
a person with deficiency resents any hints at it ;
to be sensitive to others' feelings
and avoid hitting at their Achilles' heel

0706

jau5　wun2　waa6　wun2　jau5　dip6　waa6　dip6
有碗話碗，有碟話碟

having a bowl, talk of the bowl ; having a plate, talk of a plate

實話實説，直言不諱，依照事實而言
to call a spade a spade ;
to be outspoken and honest with someone

0707

faai3 dou1 zaam2 lyun6 maa4

快刀斬亂麻

quick knife cuts off the tangled hemp

以迅捷果斷的手段，
解決錯綜複雜的問題

to cut the Gordian knot ; to grasp the nettle
– to take a quick and decisive action
to solve a complicated problem

0708

---

zau1 san1 dou1 mou5 zoeng1 lei6

周身刀冇張利

all over the body (one has) many knives, none of them sharp

每項技能都懂一點，卻無一項精通

jack of all trades, master of none

0709

---

loeng5 hip3 caap3 dou1

兩脅插刀

in two sides of rib cage stuck the knives

兩邊肋骨插上刀：比喻仗義幫忙
朋友，不怕承擔極大的犧牲

to be willing to sustain two knife wounds
for a friend – to help a friend at all
costs, even to risk one's life

0710

---

dou1 cit3 dau6 fu6 loeng5 bin1 waat6

刀切豆腐兩邊滑

(use a) knife to slice the tofu (bean curd) got two smooth sides

兩邊陣營的人都不去得罪：
比喻人處事圓滑，兩面討好

to describe someone who can be all things
to all men ; to be tactful and smooth,
pleasing different parties

0711

sik1 zi6 tau4 soeng6 jat1 baa2 dou1
色字頭上一把刀

the chinese character "salacity" is topped by a knife

比喻好色的下場可以很慘痛
being lascivious can potentially lead
to bitter consequences

0712

dou1 zai2 goe3 daai6 syu6
刀仔鋸大樹

(with) a small knife saws down a big tree

以小博大或本小利大，投資小量金錢
贏取大利潤，以小代價獲得豐厚利益
to make a big profit with just a little capital

0713

wu1 lei1 daan1 dou1
烏里單刀

Wu Lei's single saber

相傳宋末有蒙古將軍烏里，糊裏糊塗連人帶刀
墮河溺斃：引申形容人做事不倫不類、亂七八糟
to be topsy-turvy, in a complete mess, in a muddle
– it originates from a story during Song Dynasty when
a Mongol general named Wu Lei foolishly drowned
himself together with his saber and died

0714

saat3 gai1 jin1 jung6 ngau4 dou1
殺雞焉用牛刀

why kill a chicken with a beef (butcher's) knife?

辦小事情何必花大氣力
"why use a sledgehammer to crack a nut?"
– to question the use of much more force
than is needed

0715

zaam2　bang1　dou1　pek3　nau2　man4　caai4

斬崩刀劈扭紋柴

a chipped knife chopping a twisted grain firewood

難以馴服的人遇上頑劣、不聽教的人：
兩個橫蠻的人相遇，一發不可收拾；尤指婆媳衝突
two stubborn people can't get along well with one another, particularly
referring to mother and daughter-in-law conflict

0716

___

si2　haang1　gwaan1　dou1　　man4　　jau6　m4　dak1　　mou5　　jau6　m4　dak1

屎坑關刀 > 聞(文)又唔得，舞(武)又唔得

pit latrine glaive > unfit for smelling, unfit for wielding

文才和武略是古代官職的兩大技能，
若說某人不文不武，即是說他庸碌無能
to describe someone as incompetent and worthless, as he is versed in neither literary
talent nor military skills and tactics – the saying is a wordplay with two pairs of
homophones:「聞」(smell) and「文」(civil),「舞」(wield) and「武」(martial arts)

0717

117

stove.jpg

sip3 zou3 laa3
攝灶罅
fill up the stove's gap

古人會用沒用的東西填補灶罅：
現指女人嫁不出去

to describe unmarried women, spinsters – it
originates from a habit in the past when people
stuffed the gap of the stove with useless things

0718

daai6 jit6 dou2 zou3
大熱倒灶
big heat overturning the stove

本身最有機會贏的人或團隊落敗了：
結果出乎原先所預料

an unexpected loss of an odds-on favourite

0719

nin4 saam1 sap6 maan5 ze6 zou3   hou2 zou6 m4 zou6
年三十晚謝灶 ＞ 好做唔做
**on chinese new year's eve thank the stove (god)
＞ not doing what should be done (or doing what shouldn't be done)**

傳説每年年尾灶君會離開廚房回天庭述職，因此年三十晚拜謝灶君是毫無用處：
比喻人在不適當的時間或地點做不適當的事

to do the wrong thing at the wrong time,
brought by the idea that one misses the right time to worship the Stove / Kitchen God

0720

wok.jpg

daai6 wok6
大鑊
big wok

非常糟糕
a big trouble ;
to be in an awful situation

0721

me1 wok6
孭鑊
shoulder a wok

一個人或小撮人為整件錯事負責；
「孭黑鑊」即揹黑鍋，代別人受過
to be held responsible for a fault ;
another idiom "shouldering a black wok"
means to carry the can for others

0722

bou2 wok6
補鑊
mend the wok

補救失誤
damage control ;
fence-mending

0723

baau3 daai6 wok6
爆大鑊
blast a big wok

公開秘密或醜聞
to make public a big secret or scandal

0724

jat1 wok6 zuk1
一鑊粥
a wok of porridge

一塌糊塗
a big mess

0725

jat1 wok6 pou5
一鑊泡
a wok of foam

一塌糊塗
a big mess

0726

jat1 wok6 suk6
一鑊熟
a wok of cooked

全部人一齊遭殃；與人同歸於盡
everyone is caught in a bad situation
that no one can escape ;
all perish in one common ruin

0727

suk6 jan4 maai5 laan6 wok6
熟人買爛鑊
**(from) an acquaintance
bought a broken wok**

從相熟朋友那裏買到的鍋是破的：跟熟人
交易或做生意最容易受騙，又不好意思投訴
it's better not to trade with friends and
acquaintances as they would take advantage of
you and it's embarrassing to complain

0728

sin3 jat1 wok6
跣一鑊
a slip on a wok (once)

設下圈套陷害人
to pull the rug out from under someone ;
to frame or set someone up

0729

mou5 jau4 m4 lat1 dak1 wok6
冇油唔甩得鑊
**without oil, (the food) cannot
detach from the wok**

「油」指油水,「鑊」指糟糕的事:求人
辦事,不花錢則難成事;要吃點虧才能了事
it's hard to get things done without offering money
or favour ; it's necessary to suffer some losses in
order to solve the problem

0730

soeng5 dou1 saan1 lok6 jau4 wok6
上刀山落油鑊
up the hill of knives, down to the wok of hot oil

「刀山」、「油鍋」在佛教中指地獄酷刑:
比喻願意為別人吃大苦或置身險惡之地
to be prepared to suffer hardship or tread a dangerous path
for someone with determination ; come hell or high water
– brought by the idea of the harsh punishments in hell in Buddhism

0731

pot.jpg

煲 水
bou1 seoi2
boil water

「煲水新聞」一詞源自香港演藝圈，
意即炒作新聞或製造謠言
a fish story ; a hype ;
to make up fabricated news, referring to
rumours or gossips in the show business

0732

煲 劇
bou1 kek6
boil drama series

追看電視劇集
to binge-watch TV drama series

0733

煲 老 藕
bou1 lou5 ngau5
boil an old (overripe) lotus root

諷刺年輕男士找年紀老的女人談情
cougar bait - to describe a young man
who has an intimate relationship with a
middle-aged or old woman

0734

煲 電 話 粥
bou1 din6 waa2 zuk1
boil phone porridge

談了很久的電話，
像慢火煲粥般用很長的時間
to do marathon-talk on the phone ; to spend
hours on the phone just shooting the breeze

0735

125

saa1 bou1 hing1 dai6
砂煲兄弟
earthen pot brothers

從同一個砂煲裏吃飯的兄弟：
比喻一起混日子的親密朋友，
意近「同撈同煲」
brothers who eat from the same pot
– friends who work together and are
as close as brothers

0736

caak6 lou2 si3 saa1 bou1
賊佬試砂煲
the thief tests (with) an earthen pot

盜賊穿洞入屋前，先伸出砂煲扮作人頭，若煲
被敲碎即已驚動屋內人：投石問路、一探虛實
a burglar tests if there is anyone home by using a pot
– to pry about or stay speculative before taking
action ; to test the water (before doing bad things)

0737

sap6 go3 saa1 bou1 gau2 go3 goi3
十個砂煲九個蓋
ten earthen pots (having) nine lids (only)

捉襟見肘，分身不暇，兼顧不來
to describe a situation in which demand outnumbers supply ;
to fail to make ends meet ; to be inadequate for something

0738

monk.jpg

saam1　go3　wo4　soeng2　mou5　seoi2　sik6

三個和尚冇水食

three monks got no water to eat (drink)

源自民間寓言故事：「一個和尚擔水食，兩個和尚扛水食，三個和尚
冇水食。」比喻人多辦事，大家不肯互相幫助，落得一拍兩散

everybody's business is nobody's business – the proverb originates from a Chinese fable,
"one monk brings back the water by himself, two monks carry the water together, but three
monks end up getting nothing to drink." It implies the possibility that, when more people are
involved in a task, everyone tends to pass the buck, eventually nothing is accomplished

0739

---

daa2　jyun4　zaai1　m4　jiu3　wo4　soeng2

打完齋唔要和尚

after performing a rite, one doesn't want (dismisses) the monks

過橋抽板：事成之後便忘恩負義，棄用有功之人

danger past, God forgotten ; to kick someone down the ladder ;
to throw someone on the scrapheap after using him

0740

和尚擔遮 > 無髮(法)無天

wo4 soeng2 daam1 ze1 mou4 faat3 mou4 tin1

monk holding umbrella > no hair no sky (heaven)

無法無天：指不受管束，任意違反法紀和天理

to be absolutely lawless and defy justice,

as「髮」(hair) and「法」(law) are homophones in Cantonese

0741

非洲和尚 > 黑人僧(乞人憎)

fei1 zau1 wo4 soeng2 hak1 jan4 zang1 hat1

african monk > black man monk (begging people for their hatred)

黑人僧是乞人憎的諧音，意即討人厭

a loathsome or disgusting person, as the saying is

a play-on-words with two pairs of homophones:

「黑」(black) and「乞」(beg)，「僧」(monk) and「憎」(hatred)

0742

field.jpg

sau3 tin4 mou5 jan4 gaang1　gaang1 hoi1 jau5 jan4 zaang1

瘦田冇人耕，耕開有人爭

**no one tills a barren field, but once someone started
tilling it many others compete (for it)**

事情一開始沒人願意去做，但一旦有人做出成果，其他人便爭相去做

something that was first neglected for its unproductiveness is then eagerly sought
after by everyone once someone goes for it and has made some kind of achievement

0743

---

fei4 seoi2 bat1 lau4 bit6 jan4 tin4

肥水不流別人田

let not the fertile water flow into someone else's field

不要把好處給了外人

keep the goodies within the family
– benefits should not be given to nor shared with outsiders

0744

mud_&_sand.jpg

saa1 zi2

沙紙
sand paper

文憑、畢業證書。
源自英文 Cert. 的諧音
a certificate

0745

suk1 saa1

縮沙
shrinking in the sand

臨陣退縮
to chicken out ;
to get cold feet

0746

dit3 lok6 dei6 laa2 faan1 zaa6 saa1

跌落地捌番拃沙
falling on the ground but (pretending) to grab a handful of sand

嘲諷人做了錯事或糗事，為了面子而要借口掩飾；
形容人理虧也要強辯以挽回面子
to grab some sand after falling on the ground to make the fall look
like a deliberate and planned one – to tease someone who tries to save face
or cover up a cringe-making mistake by giving a poor excuse

0747

sai3 lou6 zai2 waan2 nai4 saa1
細路仔玩泥沙
children playing with sand

比喻人做事兒戲、草率不認真
to criticize someone for not taking things
seriously ; to treat a serious matter as
a child's play and work sloppily

0748

laan4 nai4 fu4 m4 soeng5 bek3
爛泥扶唔上壁
sludge cannot be plastered on a wall

朽木不可雕也：形容人資質差或不上進，
別人怎樣扶持也成不了才
you can't make a silk purse out of a sow's ear
– one can hardly turn a person who is
incompetent and unpromising into a successful man

0749

faa3 zo2 fui1 dou1 jing6 dak1 nei5
化咗灰都認得你
(even after you) became ashes I will still recognize you

對某人有很深的仇怨，誇張地指即使對方化成灰塵也能認得出來
the enmity is so deep that even the enemy dies and reduces to ashes,
one can still recognize him for revenge

0750

泥菩薩過江 > 自身難保

nai4 pou4 saat3 gwo3 gong1 / zi6 san1 naan4 bou2

a clay bodhisattva crossing the river > hardly able to save itself

形容某人已自顧不暇，更莫說去幫助別人了

to be unable to save oneself when someone is in serious trouble, let alone others ;
to be unable to help others because of one's personal difficulties

0751

泥水佬造門 > 過得自己過得人

nai4 seoi2 lou2 zou6 mun4 / gwo3 dak1 zi6 gei2 gwo3 dak1 jan4

**bricklayer builds a door > (it must be wide) enough
for himself and for others to pass through**

「過」是雙關語，有通過（一道門）和良心上過得去（對得起人）的意思：
做人做事要確保心安理得、無愧於心

one must have a clear conscience and feel no qualms for whatever he does,
so as to make the task not only acceptable to himself, but also dependable for others

0752

faeces.jpg

si2

屎

shit

糞便的俗稱：
形容技術、表現或品質差劣
crap
– to be poor in skill,
performance or quality

0753

san1 jau5 si2
身有屎
body has shit

心裏有鬼：形容人有些不可告人
的陰謀或不光彩的事
skeleton in the closet
– to describe someone having a dirty
little secret or a guilty conscience

0754

laa2 si2 soeng5 san1
揦屎上身
grab shit and put it on the body

抓起糞便沾到身上：自找麻煩
to bring trouble to oneself ;
to make a rod for one's own back

0755

gaau2 si2 gwan3
攪屎棍
stirring poop stick

喜歡興風作浪、搬弄是非、
惟恐天下不亂的麻煩製造者
a shit stirrer, a troublemaker

0756

sik6 baau2 faan6 mou5 dang2 si2 o1
食飽飯冇／等屎屙
**eaten enough rice and got no shit
to defecate / wait for shitting**

比喻人無所事事，閒得不耐煩而做些無聊事
to have nothing to do except waiting
for the call of nature – to loaf about ;
to criticize someone for doing something meaningless or
superfluous as he seems to be tired of his idle life

0757

sik6 si2 sik6 zoek6 dau6
食屎食着豆

eating shit but still found a bean to enjoy

在吃屎般的倒霉生活中仍有機會
遇見好事（豆）；沒本事的人
歪打正着，意外成功
to have found one good thing in doing a
miserable job ; to score a lucky hit

0758

daam1 si2 m4 tau1 sik6
擔屎唔偷食

while carrying shit, one wouldn't sneak a taste of it

以擔挑挑糞也不會偷食：
形容某人極之老實可靠
to sarcastically say that someone
is extremely honest

0759

jat1 daam6 saa1 tong4 jat1 daam6 si2
一啖砂糖一啖屎

a sup of granulated sugar and a sup of shit

形容一個人對另一個人時好時壞、反覆無常
to describe one's inconsistent and unpredictable treatment to another,
swinging between extremes of being sweet and nasty

0760

sou1 zau1 si2
蘇州屎
Suzhou faeces

別人遺留下來而未解決的麻煩、
爛攤子和手尾
a loose end, a problem or a mess
left over for others to follow up and fix

0761

si2 fat1 gep6 syun3 pun4
屎窟夾算盤
buttocks gripping an abacus

下接「算到盡」：
斤斤計較，不願承受一絲損失
to be petty-minded and calculating,
always haggling over every penny

0762

o1 si2 m4 ceot1 laai6 dei6 ngaang6　o1 niu6 m4 ceot1 laai6 fung1 maang5
屙屎唔出賴地硬，屙尿唔出賴風猛
unable to poop, blame the hard floor ;
unable to pee, blame the strong wind

編造牽強的藉口去為自己的過錯或失敗開脫，推卸責任
a bad workman always blames his tools
– to make a far-fetched excuse for one's own fault or failure

0763

反轉豬肚就係屎

turning a pig's stomach inside out, there is only shit

翻臉不認人：融洽的關係一旦不和便翻臉無情，
態度立刻變得惡劣或露出醜惡的一面
when falling out with someone one turns extremely hostile and nasty right away ;
to show one's true colours abruptly once the relationship turns sour

0764

龍船裝豬屎＞又長又臭

dragon boat carrying pig manure >　long and stinky

或作「懶婆紮腳布 —— 又長又臭」：
形容說話、討論或故事冗長又沒有內容
to describe a speech, discussion or story as long-winded and tedious,
sharing similar meaning with another slang expression
"lazy granny's footbinding cloth"

0765

懶人多屎尿
laan5 jan4 do1 si2 niu6

lazy people have a lot of poop and piss

懶惰的人特別多藉口偷懶
lazybones make many excuses
to slack off

0766

唔急屎唔開坑
m4 gap1 si2 m4 hoi1 haang1

(if) not in urgent need to poop, (one's) not digging a pit

或作「臨屎急開坑」,意同「現燒火現砍柴」:
平時沒準備,臨急才想辦法應付
one doesn't bother to dig a cesspit until he
is caught short – to be unprepared and
procrastinate until the last minute

0767

屎坑三姑 > 易請難送
si2 haang1 saam1 gu1　ji6 ceng2 naan4 sung3

pit latrine's 3rd aunt > easy to invite, difficult to send away

屎坑三姑是中國民間傳說中的廁神紫姑,
相傳信眾想招來紫姑問卜很易,要請她走卻很難:
形容厚臉皮、賴死不走的客人
a guest who keeps staying without any intention to leave

0768

san1 si2 haang1   saam1 jat6 hoeng1

新屎坑 〉三日香

brand new pit latrine > three-day fragrance

開始時對新的東西或興趣特別熱衷，但不久便會棄置一旁；
嘲諷人的喜好只是貪圖一時新鮮
a passing fad ; to be enthusiastic about new things
but soon get bored and abandon them only after a short while

0769

sik6 zyu1 hung4 o1 hak1 si2   maa5 soeng6 gin3 gung1

食豬紅屙黑屎 〉馬上見恭(功)

**eat pig red (blood curd), discharge black excrement
> immediately see (go to) the toilet**

「恭」是古時廁所的雅稱，取其諧音「見功」，
喻做某事情後馬上見效或引發後果
to have the desired effect or result in no time, as 「恭」(an old Chinese word
for "toilet") and 「功」(effect) are homophones in Cantonese

0770

蟧蟧瀨尿

kam4 lou2 laai6 niu6

a spider uncontrollably pees

唇瘡：蟧蟧即跳蛛，從前人們以為
唇瘡是因在睡覺時給跳蛛於唇上撒尿
cold sores – in the past it is believed that
cold sores are caused by spider pissing on
one's lips while he is sleeping

0771

屙尿都隔過渣

o1 niu6 dou1 gaak3 gwo3 zaa1

**even when pissing one still has
to filter the urine for sediments**

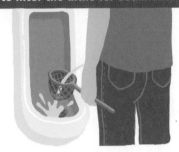

形容為人吝嗇到極點，
凡事都要計算以免他人得益
a penny-pinching Scrooge who would not
share any benefits with others

0772

天堂尿壺 〉全神貫注

tin1 tong4 niu6 wu2   cyun4 san4 gun3 zyu3

**heaven's chamber pot
> all gods pissing in (whole mind pouring in)**

注意力高度集中
to be highly concentrated and give one's full attention, as 「神」 (gods)
is a polysemous word that also means spirit and mind

0773

除褲放屁 > 多此一舉
ceoi4 fu3 fong3 pei3 > do1 ci2 jat1 geoi2

take off one's pants to fart > made an unnecessary move

做出多餘或不必要的舉動
to bring owls to Athens ;
to carry coals to Newcastle

0774

認屎認屁
jing6 si2 jing6 pei3

claiming faeces, claiming fart

自我炫耀，誇誇其談
to blow one's own trumpet
– to brag about one's own work
(which is trifling in others' eyes)

0775

一面屁
jat1 min6 pei3

a faceful of fart

被當面數落一番，
被指責得滿臉羞慚
to be yelled at or
sharply rebuked face to face

0776

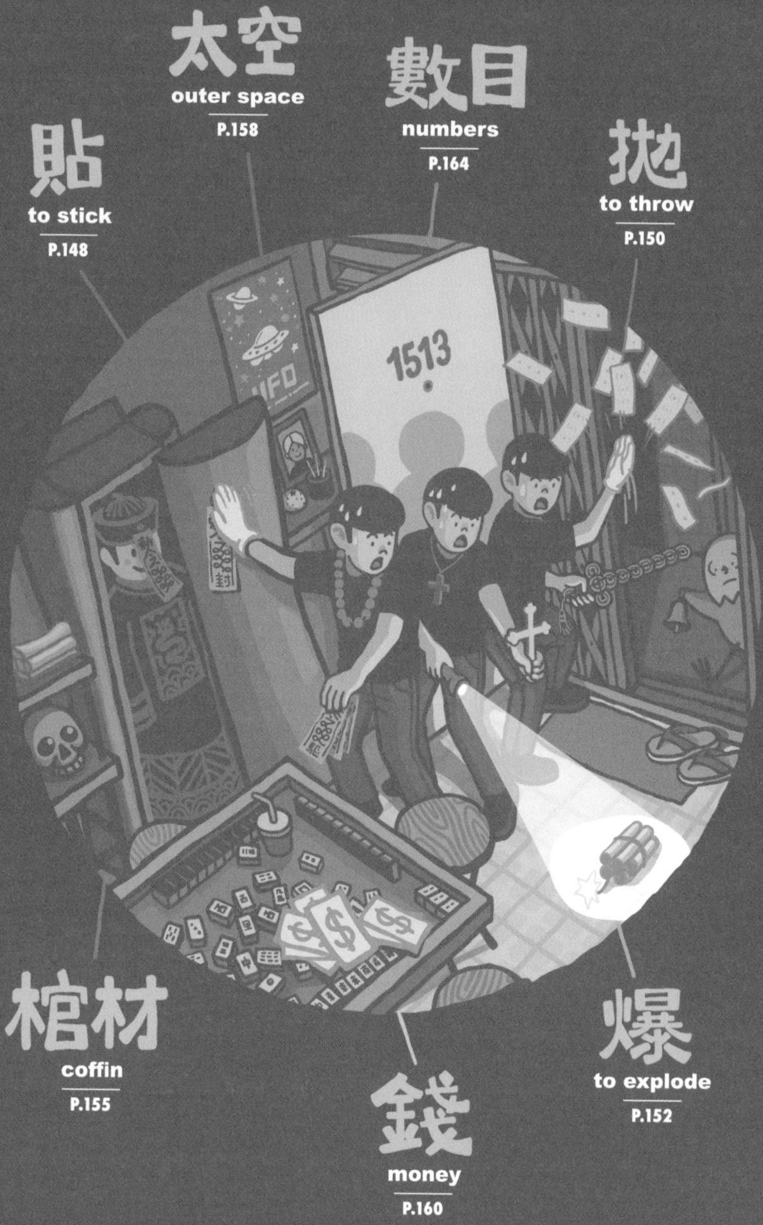
太空
outer space
P.158
數目
numbers
P.164
貼
to stick
P.148
拋
to throw
P.150
UFO
1513
棺材
coffin
P.155
爆
to explode
P.152
錢
money
P.160

to_stick.jpg

貼錯門神
tip3　co3　mun4　san4

having stuck the door gods (posters) wrong

貼門神畫像須將之以臉相對，以示齊心
守護家園，若左右對調則門神以背相對：
比喻二人意見相左，見面時互不瞅睬

to describe two persons to be at odds and not on speaking
terms with each other, as the door gods are supposed to
face one another to protect the house in a concerted effort

0777

貼身膏藥
tip3　san1　gou1　joek6

stick on body medicated plaster

總是要黏在一起、
寸步不離的情人或小孩

a clingy lover or child who needs
to be around all the time

0778

貼錢買難受
tip3　cin2　maai5　naan6　sau6

subsidizing money to buy hardship to endure

本以為付了錢可有享受或得益，
反換來了麻煩、辛勞或不好的結果

to spend money on something that unexpectedly
turns out to be one's inconvenience,
discomfort or even suffering

0779

衰到貼地
seoi1　dou3　tip3　dei2

so bad that it sticks close to the ground

某人的遭遇或現實情況倒霉透了，
差得不能再差；形容某人品格極差

to describe something that reaches the
rock bottom and cannot be worse ;
to be down on one's luck ; a nasty,
mean-spirited and ill-natured person

0780

to_throw.jpg

paau1 naau4
拋錨
throw an anchor

汽車在路上故障
to anchor ;
a roadside breakdown

0781

paau1 syu1 baau1
拋書包
throw a school bag

不必要地引經據典或咬文嚼字，
刻意賣弄自己學識廣博
to be pedantic, to unnecessarily quote
literary classics or references to
make a display of one's erudition

0782

paau1 long6 tau4
拋浪頭
throw a wave

虛張聲勢嚇唬對方，
讓人高估自己的實力而退讓
to bluff and bluster ;
to try to scare someone off
with a feigned show of strength

0783

daai6 paau1 wo4
大拋禾
a big throw of standing grain

無能而又靠不住的窩囊廢
a wuss who is incompetent
and good at nothing

0784

to_explode.jpg

baau3　sek6
爆 石
blast rock

用炸藥炸開石頭或山頭；排便
rock blasting ; to defecate

0785

baau3　gaak3
爆 格
blast a square frame

破門爆竊，音譯自英文 burgle
a transliteration of the English word "burgle"

0786

baau3　bou1
爆 煲
blast pot

負荷或壓力太大，超出了限度
a pressure-cooker atmosphere ;
to describe something or someone
to be overloaded and about to collapse

0787

baau3　gong1
爆 缸
blast (water) tank

受傷而流血
to bleed (like a leaking tank)

0788

baau3 taai1
爆 呔
burst tyre

輪胎洩氣；褲子撕襠
tyre punctures ;
to get one's trousers split open accidentally

0789

---

baau3 dang1
爆 燈
blast lamp

厲害到極點
to be incredibly awesome

0790

---

baau3 tou5
爆 肚
burst belly

表演時不依劇本，
即興創作台詞或歌詞
to improvise and ad-lib in a play,
a speech or a singing performance

0791

---

baau3 hoeng2 hau2
爆 響 口
blasting loud mouth

將不該說出來的私事或秘密公諸於世
to leak a secret ;
to blow the lid off something

0792

coffin.jpg

gun1 coi4 bun2
棺材本
the capital for a coffin

給自己買棺材安葬的錢，
借指儲起來養老送終的本錢
a retirement pension or life savings
for one's living at his old age (or for the
expenses of his own funeral)

0793

maai5 gun1 coi4 m4 zi1 deng6
買棺材唔知埞
don't know where to buy a coffin

形容人不知死活，意識不到自己的舉動
很危險，或不知好歹得罪有勢力的人
to act recklessly, to be heedless of danger ;
to be completely unaware of the fact that one
may have offended some influential people

0794

m4 gin3 gun1 coi4 m4 lau4 ngaan5 leoi6
唔見棺材唔流眼淚
not until one sees his own coffin does one shed tears

比喻人大難臨頭卻毫無危機感，不感害怕
to be oblivious to danger ;
to yield at the eleventh hour in the face of the grim reality

0795

man4 dou2 gun1 coi4 hoeng1
聞到棺材香
having scented the coffin's fragrance

行將就木，年老之人將要死亡
to have one foot in the grave

0796

deng1 goi3
釘蓋
nail the lid (of one's coffin)

釘上棺木的蓋，意即死亡
to be dead

0797

toi4 gun1 coi4 lat1 fu3 sat1 lai5 sei2 jan4
抬棺材甩褲 〉失禮死人
**(when) lifting up a coffin one dropped his pants
> being rude to the dead people**

非常失禮
a faux pas, a gaffe ; to have dropped a clanger - as 「死」 (dead) in Cantonese
can also be used as an adverb meaning "deadly, extremely"

0798

outer_space.jpg

zo2 zyu6 dei6 kau4 zyun3

阻住地球轉

hinder Earth from rotating

黑人阻礙某事情或工作的進展，
影響正常運作
to get in the way of something ; to obstruct
the progress of someone else's matter

0799

fo2 sing1 zong6 dei6 kau4

火星撞地球

Mars collides with Earth

兩個性情剛烈的人或強隊走在一起，
定必迸發激烈火花和衝突，難以協作
a clash between two persons of strong
personalities or two powerful groups ;
to describe two uncooperative or incompatible
parties working together

0800

sou3 baa2 sing1

掃把星

broom star

彗星；
帶來厄運與不幸的人
a comet ;
a hoodoo or jinx who brings bad luck

0801

zaa1 fo2 zin3

揸火箭

driving rocket

考試拿到甲等成績，因A字外形似
火箭，或含「成績步步高升」之意
to have A grades in exams,
as "A" shapes like a rocket

0802

jim4　cin2　seng1
嫌錢腥
disrelish money's fishy smell

不像其他人般對金錢感興趣；
嫌惡不義之財
to show no interest in money ;
to refuse filthy lucre

0803

faat3　cin2　hon4
發錢寒
catch a cold (have a fever) for money

形容人很愛錢、見錢開眼，
即使很小的金額也要拿到手
to crave money, to be money hungry
or money-obsessed

0804

sak1　cin2　jap6　nei5　doi2
塞錢入你袋
stuff money in your pocket

免費給你上一課，
教懂你一些做人的道理
to hospitably give someone a life lesson ;
to teach someone something for free

0805

zaan6　cin2　maai5　faa1　daai3
賺錢買花戴
earn money to buy flowers to wear

主要形容某些女性並非家庭的主要
經濟支柱，工作只為賺取額外的餘錢
to describe some women who go to work
only for earning spare cash for inessentials,
as they are not the breadwinners

0806

dong3 gaau1 hok6 fai3
當交學費
think of it as paying tuition fees

學習某種賭博或炒賣，輸錢當作
繳學費；給騙取了金錢，就當買個教訓
to take one's financial loss, being a beginner in
gambling or investment, as tuition fee paid ; to consider
the experience of being defrauded as a lesson learnt

0807

hung1 tau4 zi1 piu3
空頭支票
blank (bounced) cheque

許下不會實踐的承諾
an empty or wild promise

0808

gung1 gung6 din6 waa2　mou5 cin2 mou5 dak1 king1
公共電話 > 冇錢冇得傾
public phone > no money no talk

沒錢免談
to emphasize that money is the only thing that matters now,
further discussion is only possible if it is profitable

0809

cyun1 gwai6 tung2 dai2
穿櫃桶底
bore through the drawer's bottom

把存錢的抽屜弄穿：
意即偷去僱主的錢財，或虧空公款
embezzlement ;
to steal money from one's employer

0810

sat1 si4 gaap3 maan6
失匙夾萬
lost key safe

夾萬內有錢卻拿不到：
雖是富家子弟，卻不能掌控家族財產
a rich person, esp. the second generation
of the rich, who does not have access to his
family wealth

0811

bo1 lei1 gaap3 maan6　jau5 dak1 tai2 mou5 dak1 sai2
玻璃夾萬 > 有得睇冇得使
glass safe > one can see (the money) but cannot use it

東西能看卻不能用或不管用；
或比喻固定資產不能隨時動用
to describe something that looks good but is not practical or usable ;
to speak of the fixed assets which cannot be easily converted into cash
and drawn on, as compared to the current assets

0812

numbers.jpg

baat3

八

eight

源自「諸事八卦」，古時的人遇事必
不勝其煩地卜卦，後引申形容人好管閒事，
愛打聽別人隱私；作動詞用即為打聽消息
to be nosy or meddlesome ; a busybody who always
gossips about people ; to pry into something
– it originates from "bagua" the eight trigrams
which people use to consult an oracle

0813

jat1　ng5　jat1　sap6

一五一十

one (every) five one (every) ten

五和十是計算單位，即五個十個地
點清數目：比喻原原本本、
從頭到尾無遺漏地敍述
to narrate systematically and in full detail,
as five and ten are the counting units

0814

---

ji6　daa2　luk6

二打六

two beats six

原指戲班裏的閒角，引申指無關
重要的小人物，或用以貶低人
未夠斤両或資格
a flunky or an unimportant person ; a phrase
used to disparage someone, asserting that
he is inferior or incompetent

0815

---

saam1　coeng4　loeng5　dyun2

三長兩短

three long two short

原指棺木的三長板與二短板
（不計棺蓋），引申指遭逢不測、
意外的變故以致身亡
unforeseen disasters or accidents ;
unexpected misfortune that leads to one's death

0816

---

saam1　fan1　zung1　jit6　dou6

三分鐘熱度

three-minute heat (passion)

短暫的熱衷，對事物很快失去興趣
to have a brief period of
enthusiasm and give up halfway ;
a passing fancy

0817

gong2 loi4 gong2 heoi3 saam1 fuk1 pei3

講來講去三幅被

keep talking over and over about the three quilts

下接「度嚟度去二丈四」：
說來說去都是重複、毫無新意的老話題
to harp on about the same subject ;
to sound like a broken record

0818

---

m4 saam1 m4 sei3

唔三唔四

neither three nor four

說人背景不好、不正經；
奇奇怪怪、不正當的東西或地方
to describe a person who is not of good
background ; to describe things or places
as odd and improper

0819

gang2 geng2 sei3

梗頸四

stiff-neck four

殿軍：在比賽中得到第四名，
跟三甲擦肩而過，難免有點不服氣
the third runner-up
– one may feel bitter or regretful as he is
considered to have lost the game

0820

aa3 sei3
阿四
ah four

家中的傭人；任人差遣的人：從前富戶會僱用
近身、洗熨、煮飯和雜務的四種傭工，但小戶人
家只能僱一個人包辦四項工作，故稱為「阿四」
a house servant or domestic worker ; a person
who is ordered around to do menial tasks

0821

ng5 ng5 bo1
五五波
five five ball

機率一半一半；比賽中雙方
勢均力敵，勝出的機會均等
a fifty-fifty chance ;
two teams are well matched in a game

0822

cin4 cat1
錢七
money seven

殘舊不堪的車：殘舊的汽車引擎轉動時，
會產生「錢七錢七」的聲音
a shabby old car (an onomatopoeia
imitating the sound an old car's engine makes)

0823

mak6 cat1
墨七
ink seven

鼠摸：夜間作案的小偷
a burglar or thief
who steals things at night time

0824

bun3 gan1 baat3 loeng2

半斤八兩

half a catty Vs. eight taels

兩者相當，彼此不相上下，不相伯仲
six of one, half a dozen of the other ;
to be well-matched
– as one catty equals sixteen taels

0825

gau2 m4 daap3 baat3

九唔搭八

nine doesn't match eight

牛頭不對馬嘴：答非所問；
說話不着邊際，離題，胡扯
an entirely irrelevant response ;
to talk nonsense, total gibberish

0826

m4 lei5 saam1 cat1 ji6 sap6 jat1

唔理三七二十一

not giving a damn about the three seven twenty-one

甚麼也不管了：不問是非情由（先做了算）
anyway, no matter what
(to act first regardless of causes or consequences)

0827

屈尾十
wat1 mei5 sap6

bending tail ten

忽然掉頭離開；突然間改變主意
或出爾反爾，令人措手不及
to suddenly turn around and walk away ;
to have a sudden change of mind and go back
on one's word (which may imply betrayal)

0828

十五十六
sap6 ng5 sap6 luk6

fifteen sixteen

忐忑不安，猶豫不決
to be indecisive,
to vacillate over something

0829

受人二分四
sau6 jan4 ji6 fan1 sei3

receiving 2 candareens & 4 (cash)

下接「做到一肚氣/索晒氣」，「二分四」
是清末時期的日薪，收了人錢便要做到
筋疲力盡：比喻自己受僱於人，即使
工錢微薄，做到一肚子氣也只能忍受
one has to work hard or suck it up as he is paid for it
as an employee after all, even at a very low wage

0830

亂噏廿四
lyun6 ngap1 jaa6 sei3

messily speaking twenty-four

24 是「易死」的諧音，因人們忌諱談死，
故不能隨便亂說：引申形容人胡說八道
to talk bullshit - as in Cantonese "24"
sounds like 「易死」(die easily)
which is a taboo conversation topic

0831

m4 paa3 jat1 maan6　zi3 paa3 maan6 jat1
唔怕一萬 至怕萬一
not afraid of ten thousand, but afraid of one-ten-thousandth

只怕遇上意外，哪怕是萬分一機率的可能性：
人總要準備好應急措施
just in case ; one should be prepared for any contingencies
and always have a contingency plan

0832

---

sap6 waak6 dou1 mei6 jau5 jat1 pit3
十劃都未有一撇
(in) ten strokes, not yet one left-falling stroke

事情毫無眉目，一點成事的跡象也未見，現在言之過早
things have not even begun to take shape ;
it's too soon to tell as there is not the slightest sign of anything happening yet

0833

足球
football
P.178

茶餐廳
Hong Kong style cafe
P.174

籃球
basketball
P.182

職場
workplace
P.184

Jargons 術語

茶餐廳

Hong Kong style cafe

leng3 zai2
靚仔
handsome boy

一碗白飯：
因為淨白飯只得白色，
有如青靚白淨的男子
plain rice, as rice is white which is
like a fair-skinned guy

0834

leng3 neoi2
靚女
pretty girl

一碗白粥：
由白飯被稱為「靚仔」引申而來
plain rice porridge, deriving from
calling plain rice the "handsome boy"

0835

sai3 jung2
細蓉
small lotus

雲吞麵：
源於其別稱「芙蓉面（麵）」，喻意精緻靚麵
有如美人面容；較大的分量為「大蓉」
wonton noodles, originating from a metaphor used to
describe a girl's face that is as beautiful as lotus, as
"face" and "noodles" are homophones in Cantonese

0836

daa2 laan6
打爛
beat to break

炒飯：
因蛋炒飯需要先打爛雞蛋
fried rice, as one needs to break
eggs for cooking fried rice

0837

zau2　ceng1

走青
runaway green

湯粉麵不要加蔥、
芫荽或其他青菜配料
a requesting remark of not adding spring
onion or Chinese parsley in the noodles

0838

---

zau2　tim4

走甜
runaway sweetness

飲品不要加糖
a requesting remark of not adding
sugar in the beverages

0839

---

zau2　sik1

走色
runaway colour

食物不要加豉油或者肉汁
a requesting remark of not adding
soy sauce or gravy in the dishes

0840

---

fei1　saa1　zau2　naai5

飛沙走奶
flying sands and runaway milk

咖啡不要砂糖和花奶，即齋啡
black coffee with
no sugar or milk added

0841

fei4 mui1
肥妹
fat girl

熱巧克力：因是高熱量飲品，
多喝會致肥，故有此戲稱
hot chocolate, as it is a high-calorie drink
which makes people gain weight

0842

sik6 baa3 wong4 caan1
食霸王餐
eat an overlord's meal

用餐後故意不付錢，白吃白喝
dine and dash

0843

daa2 baau1
打包
beat and wrap

把在餐廳吃不完的食物包好拿回家
to take leftovers home in a doggie bag

0844

haang4 gaai1
行街
walking in the street

外賣，包括自取或速遞送外賣
food delivery or take-away

0845

football

ji1 jyun2 bo1
醫院波
hospital ball

容易令接應隊友受傷的傳球，例如將
對方球員引向隊友搶截，令隊友受傷；
引申指不到位、不恰當的傳球
hospital pass – a pass that subjects the
recipient to heavy contact, usually unavoidable,
from an opposing player

0846

hoeng1 ziu1 bo1
香蕉波
banana ball

弧旋球或弧線球：
使球作弧線運行的腳法
banana kick,
shots that curl or swerve

0847

sik6 bo1 beng2
食波餅
eat ball cake

被球擊中面部
to be hit by a ball in one's face

0848

caai2 bo1 ce1
踩波車
step on the ball car

不小心踏在球上而失平衡跌倒
to have stumbled or stepped
on the ball and fall down

0849

tung1 haang1 keoi4

通坑渠

clear the drainage

運球時把球於對手兩腳之間推過

nutmeg, tunnel
– to play the ball through
the legs of an opponent

0850

---

ding2 tau4 ceoi4

頂頭鎚

butt the head hammer

用頭頂球

header
– to control the ball using one's head
to pass, shoot or clear

0851

---

caau2 fei1 gei1

炒飛機

fry the aeroplane

射門高出目標很多

a shot that goes far above the goal

0852

---

taan4 pei4 paa2

彈琵琶

play pipa (Chinese lute)

守門員甩手而抱不住對方的射球，
把球彈了出來，甚至入了龍門

to describe a goalkeeper who catches the ball
but fails to hold it tight, letting it bounce out
of his grasp or even get into the goal

0853

caap3　seoi2
插水
enter (dive into) the water

假摔：球員為博取罰球，假裝被對手
侵犯而倒地，動作像跳水而得名
diving, simulation, flopping – a player's attempt
to gain an unfair advantage by falling to the
ground and possibly feigning an injury

0854

aau2　caai4
拗柴
twisted firewood

足踝扭傷
an ankle sprain

0855

mo4　goeng1
磨薑
grate the ginger

在石地踢波時，腳部與地面
磨擦而造成損傷
friction burns on feet caused by rubbing
against the floor when playing
on a concrete pitch

0856

caau2　gaai3　laan2
炒芥蘭
fry the Chinese kale

兩個球員的腿部碰在一起及撞傷
a leg-to-leg collision
between two players

0857

basketball

caap3　faa1
插花
insert (arrange) flowers

胯下運球
between-the-legs dribble

0858

---

jap6　zoen1
入樽
put into the bottle

灌籃或扣籃：球員躍起把球放進
籃框內，隨後或會短暫抓着籃框
slam dunk – a shot performed
by a player who jumps and thrusts
the ball down through the basket

0859

---

cyun1　zam1
穿針
thread a needle

空心球：投籃時籃球不觸及籃框
或籃板而直接進球
clean shot, nothing but net – a perfect
shot that goes through the basket without
touching the rim or backboard

0860

---

dap6　deng1
揼釘
hammer the nail

投籃時籃球因撞到籃框
而彈開，進不了球
a missed shot of which the ball hits the rim
of the basket and bounces out

0861

workplace

paau2 sou3

跑數
run the numbers

員工拼命達到某個銷售目標
或業務指標，最常見於推銷業
to sweat blood to meet one's quota
or sales goal

0862

---

zeot1 sou3

捽數
rub the numbers

上司要求及督促下屬於限期內達
到某銷售目標或業務指標
to describe a supervisor cracking the whip,
urging a subordinate to meet his sales target

0863

---

duk1 sou3

篤數

poke the numbers

造假賬，報大數據
to cook the books ; window dressing
in accounting which involves
an exaggeration of positive data

0864

---

sou3 baa2

掃把
broom

主管：
源自英文 Supervisor 的諧音
supervisor – as "sou ba"
sounds like "super"

0865

射波
se6 bo1
shoot the ball

指職員詐病或借故請假；音近
「卸膊」；放假將工作交予同事，
又似球員將波射給隊友
to malinger for sick leave from work

0866

A字膊
zi6 bok3
"A" character (A-shape) shoulder

形容人經常卸膊，即規避責任，
或推卸責任予他人
to describe someone who always shirks
his duty or passes the buck to others

0867

篤背脊
duk1 bui3 zek3
poke (one's) back

打小報告，在別人背後
以言語中傷其人
to backstab and bad-mouth someone ;
to tattle on someone

0868

收大信封
sau1 daai6 seon3 fung1
receive a big envelope

收到解僱信，即被解僱
to have received a termination letter ;
to get the sack

0869

mau1 dan1
踎 墩
squat down at the mound

指失業：「墩」即舊時船隻卸貨之處，
搬運苦力失業時，便會蹲在碼頭等待新工作
being unemployed – as "mound" refers to the cargo
loading port in the past, where the unemployed
coolies squatted to wait for new jobs

0870

loeng4 dei6
量 地
measure the land

即「度來度去（踱來踱去）」：
形容人失業無所事事
to be idle and walk to and fro purposelessly as
one is unemployed, as「度」(measure) and
「踱」(pace) are homophones in Cantonese

0871

zaa1 dau1
揸 兜
hold a (beggar's) bowl

淪落至乞食：因沒有工作而貧困
an exaggerated expression of a person
becoming extremely poor due to unemployment,
as if he needs to beg after losing his job

0872

tiu3 cou4
跳 槽
jump (to another) trough

轉職
to change one's job

0873

參考書目及網頁
References

歐陽覺亞、周無忌、饒秉才（編著），《廣州話俗語詞典》。香港：商務印書館，2009

盧譚飛燕（編譯），《廣州話口語詞彙》。香港：中文大學出版社，2007
LO TAM Fee-yin, *Cantonese Colloquial Expressions*
The Chinese University Press, Hong Kong, 2007

蘇紹興（編譯），《英譯廣州話常用口語詞匯》。香港：中文大學出版社，2011
SO Simon Siu-hing, *A Glossary of Common Cantonese Colloquial Expressions*
The Chinese University Press, Hong Kong, 2011

饒原生，《港粵口頭禪趣解》。香港：洪波出版，2007

粵語審音配詞字庫（香港語言學學會注音系統）
Chinese Character Database (Transcription System : LSHK)
(With Word-formations, Phonologically Disambiguated According to the Cantonese Dialect)

humanum.arts.cuhk.edu.hk/Lexis/lexi-can/

CantoDict

www.cantonese.sheik.co.uk/dictionary/

粵典

words.hk/zidin/

廣府話小研究：大粵港諺語
Blog of Cantonese Resources：Cantonese Proverbs in One Picture

writecantonese8.wordpress.com/2014/02/25/cantonese-proverbs-in-one-picture/

粵拼索引
Jyutping Index

Cantonese2.jpg

編　繪	阿塗	**Author** : Ah To
翻　譯	七刻	**Translator** : Chukhak
出版經理	Fokaren	**Publishing Manager** : Fokaren
編　輯	七刻	**Editor** : Chukhak
校　對	阿珊（英文文稿）	**Proofreader** : Ah Shan (Eng. text)
	阿戴、阿峻、阿田、阿雞	Ah Daai, Ah Zeon, Ah Tin, Ah Gai
美術監督	sunnysunshine	**Art Director** : sunnysunshine
書籍設計	阿塗	**Book Designer** : Ah To

出　版　白油出版
白卷出版社
黑紙有限公司
新界葵涌大圓街 11–13 號
同珍工業大廈 B 座 1 樓 5 室

網　址　www.whitepaper.com.hk
電　郵　email@whitepaper.com.hk

發　行　泛華發行代理有限公司
電　郵　gccd@singtaonewscorp.com
版　次　2018 年 7 月初版
2018 年 10 月第二版
2020 年 1 月第三版
2020 年 12 月第四版
2023 年 7 月第五版

I S B N　978–988–79042–7–4

Whitepaper Publishing

Blackpaper Limited

Unit 5, 1/F, Block B,

Tung Chun Industrial Building

11-13 Tai Yuen Street,

Kwai Chung

website : www.whitepaper.com.hk

email : email@whitepaper.com.hk

Circulated by Global China Circulation & Distribution Ltd

email : gccd@singtaonewscorp.com

First published in July 2018

Second edition published in October 2018

Third edition published in January 2020

Fourth edition published in December 2020

Fifth edition published in July 2023

I S B N 978-988-79042-7-4